FACING THE DARKNESS

(Rhonda's Story)

Chane' Lucas

Author

Enhanced DNA Publishing
Indianapolis Indiana

Chane' Lucas

FACING THE DARKNESS
(Rhonda's Story)

ISBN-13: 978-1-7334198-6-4

DEDICATION

In loving memory of my Goddaughter
Shayna Olivia Wilcox and to all those who were a part of
my process and growth.

INTRODUCTION

This novel is for the broken. When you find yourself staring your past in the face, a moment comes when you must choose to release it and find the Grace to live, knowing that you can! You can live your best life on purpose! There is help for you and I hope this book will challenge you to face the things you have suffered and endured. Remember there is always help, loved ones, friends and even those who have more wisdom on life then you. Learn to receive help and the love of those placed in your life. Those who are there to assist you as you walk through the dark places of your past, knowing the future is for you and it can be bright as the Son!

To those who have encouraged me, I never would have been in this place without you! I would like to list a few people I want to thank. First my mother and father who taught me where to go when things get hard in life. My sister who taught me how to get there and has been my biggest encourager in so many ways. My pre-editors who stayed on me, held me accountable of my time and pushed me to tears. My mentor and greatest encourager who told me I was made for this now own it! My leaders who encouraged me, guided me, never judged me, built me over the years, cared for me as a mother and father away from my eternal home. You all inspire me and give me everything I have needed to make this possible.

Most of all, I cannot thank my Creator enough for placing this novel within me and giving me the Grace to bring it into the atmosphere. I give you all Glory and Honor for this and I pray it serves your purpose and gives life to the dead places people walk through and can't find a place to release it. Let these words bring them to you that you may receive the Glory which is due your Name.

Facing the Darkness (Rhonda's Story)

TABLE OF CONTENTS

TRUSTING THROUGH BROKENNESS

Rushing through an open doorway, Rhonda found herself staring down a long hallway. High heel, black boots and a short skirt, with pins holding the zipper up strutting her long legs as fast as she could, given her panic-stricken heart. A bit tattered and tired from a long day of working at the "Exclusive" restaurant. She was lucky Michelle just happened to come in early, when she got the call and offered to cover the remainder of her shift for the evening. Michelle was a good friend like that, she had a special knack for showing up just in the nick of time.

As Rhonda made her way down the hall, mocha complexion was glistening from the almost jogging she was doing to reach her destination. She could see all the colorful pictures placed ever so closely together, as if to ensure there was no space left unused. Wondering to herself if any of them were from her child. As the thought faded, she found herself at the end of the hallway, repeating to herself, "go left, then right or was it, go right then left." Yes, Rhonda was lost on a one-way hall. Truth is, she had never even been to her daughter's school before this day, aside from enrollment, and would not be here now, if it weren't for the call she received from Mr. Thompson, the school counselor. A call, which had her all turned around and in an uproar about the welfare of "Ami."

Rhonda could hardly think clearly, she had become so frustrated and concerned for Ami. As she turned to revisit the lane she had just come down, she realized she had passed a hallway positioned to her left. She had been so busy strolling the corridor looking at the neatly positioned drawings high on the wall, she had forgotten to look around for the correct path as she walked. Retracing her steps, trying to remember the directions Mr. Thompson had given, she took the hallway which was to her left and heard a male voice, "May I be of assistance?" Thinking to herself sarcastically, "yeah, like five minutes ago!", she mumbled under her breath, "Yes, I'm looking for the nurse's office."

The man, dressed in an oversized sports jacket of orange and brown, sporting what some would think a toupee, when in fact, it was just the way he wore his natural hair. He glared at her, looking a bit puzzled, "How did you get, in, here?" he asked in confusion. "The nurse's office is on the other side of the building. Go right then left to the next hallway," he quickly stated. A bit agitated, Rhonda turned toward the man and rolled her slightly large hazel colored eyes, "Never mind, how I got in here. The problem now is, I'm lost!" The man seeing her frustration kindly stated, "Here ma'am, let me escort you there, make sure you find it." "Thank you!" she exclaimed. Making their way down the hall and to the right, she found herself feeling a bit overwhelmed by all the different twists and turns he began to take her on. Thinking to herself, "There is no way I would've found my way out of here, I don't even know how I got in."

Finally reaching their destination, she was dropped at a desk where a short-framed lady sat, "Here we are ma'am, the nurse's office." Rhonda looked around the room which was almost as if it was a check-in at a hospital emergency room. It was filled with all the different gadgets used to check vitals of someone being admitted to a hospital. Seemed rather strange to have all these things for some elementary school children, "Never mind all that," she thought to herself, "Hey, I'm Rhonda Hodge, here to pick up my daughter Ami Bayt." "Your relation ma'am?" the lady from behind the counter questioned, as she peered over her glasses at Rhonda. "Her Mother!" Sensing the frustration in her voice, the lady politely rose from the chair directing Rhonda to follow her, she quickly said, "This way ma'am." Rhonda's statue of 6 feet one inch alone could be intimidating, not to mention her face always appeared angry, even when she was having a good day. Life for Rhonda had been hard as a single mother, especially with no family she could turn to when times seemed too hard.

As Rhonda entered the room, a smile came over her face when she spotted Ami. She was positioned in the middle of a cot as if she was a character in a story book. Surrounded by plush stuffed animals, holding on to a breathing mask, it looked as if she was being given oxygen to sustain her life. With pitiful eyes, she looked up and spoke through the mask, "Mommy!" Rhonda's heart fell to the pit of her stomach. She had not expected to find Ami in this state. She rushed over to her, sat on the cot, and hugged her tightly. A woman walked in the room wearing a white coat, and for a moment, Rhonda forgot she was in a school. Thinking to herself, "What kind of glorified situation have I stepped into?" She was feeling as if she had stepped into an episode of the twilight zone. "Ms. Hodge," the woman questioned softly, "I am Stacy Leddy, the school Practitioner. How are you?" as she sanitized her hands and stepped closer to the cot they were sitting on. "I'm fine, thank you for asking, but what is going on with my daughter? Why does she have this mask on her face?" Rhonda asked in confusion.

Rhonda was already feeling a bit flustered from the long walk, rude looks, not to mention, getting up at 4 am to get herself ready for work and Ami off to her before school daycare. All of this was a bit too much. Feeling a bit emotional from what she was seeing around her and the mask on Ami's face, Rhonda's eyes began to fill with tears. "Ms. Hodge, Ami gave us quite a scare. She collapsed in recess and was unable to catch her breath." Mrs. Leddy stated. "We did get her calmed down and were able to give her two breathing treatments."

"I am assuming the school counselor obtained your permission?" Mrs. Leddy stated. "Yes, but I didn't really understand all he was trying to say, so I just said yeah." Rhonda said annoyingly. "Well, it seems Ami has had an onset of Asthma. How do you have an onset of Asthma?" Rhonda replied sharply. "She has never had any trouble with recess before, that I know of?"

"Well, recess is not the problem, it's her lungs." Mrs. Leddy sharply stated as she looked down at Rhonda's clothing and boots. "She will need to see her physician and be treated with a regimen of asthma medications, like these treatments, until her asthma is under control." Looking at Rhonda once more, with a look of uncertainty, Mrs. Leddy quickly stated, "Ami does have a Primary Care Physician, doesn't she?" As if to say from the looks of Rhonda it wouldn't be something she would keep up with or be concerned about.

Rhonda, feeling judged, opened her mouth to speak, when a gentleman entered the room, "Umm..." Suddenly being interrupted, which she was glad of, because she didn't want to tell Mrs. Leddy that Ami had not been to the doctor in a year. Rhonda had been promoted at her job and stayed so busy she had not had the time to schedule checkups. She signed up for the insurance, but she didn't stop to even question if her health insurance had become effective yet. "Hi, I'm Mr. Thompson, I assume your Ms. Hodge, we spoke on the phone." Reaching his hand out to Rhonda and giving it a firm shake, he turned to Ami, "and how are you feeling now, young lady?"

Ami, with the mask in her hand, attached to her face, as if she was still having a treatment, but the truth is, she liked the adventure of the mask. The machine had run out about five minutes before Mrs. Leddy walked in. "I feel ok," She replied, as she looked at the machine, wondering why the smoke had stopped, giving the mask a good shake but never removing it from her face. "Well, I think we can let you go home now, young lady." Mrs. Leddy stated. Rhonda, remembering the question she was asked, felt relief as she stood and grabbed her purse she had placed in the chair.

Noticing the man looking her up and down as if in displeasure of her dress, she turned, looking uncomfortable and said, "Thank you. Where do I get her school stuff?" Mr. Thompson realizing the expression on his face had caused Rhonda's disposition, replied with a quirky smile. "If the two of you would follow me, I will escort you to her classroom," he directed with his hand. "Mrs. Allen has everything ready for you," he continued.

"Making their way to Mrs. Allen's classroom, Mr. Thompson opened the door. A quirky little lady jumped from her chair and rushed towards the company of people. "Oh Ami," she sighed, "Are you ok now?" With heartfelt concern she questioned, as she leaned over hugging Ami and looking at Rhonda with eyes of amazement. "Ami is a very bright young lady, I hope she will be back with us tomorrow, in tip top shape!" She exclaimed, quirkily. "Well, here are her things..." she nervously whispered, as she walked over and grabbed a ratty little sweater and bookbag which had received its wear for worse, months ago.

"Thank you." Rhonda replied. "Well Ami let's go," she said

sharply, grabbing her things and turning to Mr. Thompson with an 'I'm over this' look on her face, she said, now gritting her teeth from all the be judging looks, "Mr. Thompson, could you show me the way out of here?" "Oh, Mrs. Bayt, Ami's study lessons and homework." Rhonda, turning with a quick spin, "That's, Ms. Hodge," she said in a huff. "Oh, I'm extremely sorry!" "My apologies." Mrs. Allen said, with her head shifted down toward the floor. Rhonda could tell Mrs. Allen was a very humble women and didn't mean any harm, however all the stares and comments left her feeling less than she could have imagined. She almost felt sorry for how she behaved until she remembered the stares of those she had just met. Now all she wanted to do was get Ami and herself out of there.

As they made their way to the exit and out the door, Rhonda felt a bit embarrassed and frustrated more than usual by this time. Ami stopped to catch her breath. Rhonda realizing this was a bit more serious then she had anticipated from the previous events, stopped to check on Ami. "It's ok, baby. I'm going to get you home and you can lay down. Everything will be just fine." The fear in her voice was evident, as the words trembled from her mouth. She had never seen Ami like this and wasn't certain what she would do.

Rhonda, unsure how she was going to cover expenses if she had to take Ami to the hospital, wondered if her new policy would have already taken effect. Michelle had gotten her this new position just about six months prior and it was going to be very hard to take a day or two off to monitor Ami, in fact she felt it would be impossible. Not to mention the expense if she had medications to cover, she was just getting to a place where she felt financially stable. This was a great position, but it wouldn't take much at this point, for her to be back in a whole lot of debt again.

Finally making their way to the car and getting Ami all settled in the seat, she began to start the car. Pushing the key into the ignition she turned to Ami and said, "Good old car, we have come real far, crank for me now baby, and be the star!" This is something she said as her good luck charm. Truth is, the car was old and rusted, with no muffler and had exhaust coming in from the backseat floorboard. Everything on it was falling apart, including the steering wheel which was taped together in more than one area with duct tape. She began to realize the car may be a problem for Ami, with her having trouble breathing already. She started the car and hoped for the best. "Are you ok, baby?" Ami nodded her head, "Yes," as she placed the car in gear and began to drive off.

Replaying the events of the morning, Rhonda knew Ami wasn't herself when she found her still asleep when she went into her room to wake her this morning. Not yet realizing the seriousness of the situation she was facing, as she knew nothing about asthma onsets, she began to think to herself "Why didn't she tell me she really wasn't feeling good?" Rhonda also replayed the events she encountered with the school officials. "How dare she look at me like that!" "They aren't no better than me, lookin' at me like I don't work just as hard, if not harder than they do!" She thought to herself. Ami, feeling the anger brewing within her mother by the expression on her face, closed her eyes and tried not to think about the trouble she had caused her mother. Besides, her chest hurt more than she had let on and she wasn't about to tell her mother at that point.

Rhonda made her way to the door of the building, "Ami, are you feeling that bad?" "Come on here. Let's get you inside to rest! I still have to get dinner started and wash your uniforms for school tomorrow, I'm sure all you need is just to lay down for a while!" She yelled from the doorway of the apartment building trying to pretend the situation was less serious. This was just the way Rhonda had learned to deal with the hard places, suck it up and keep it moving. Lord knows she had her share of them in the past and she wasn't about to let this event take over her or Ami's life.

At this point Ms. Nosey was at the peep whole peering through as if she had no business of her own, "It's just Me and Ami, Ms. No...Johnson" as the door of her apartment made its normal noises from her leaning against it to peep.

As Rhonda held the door open for Ami, she noticed she was much sicker than she imagined, yet she didn't think to help her up the stairs into the complex. She was raising Ami to be strong and not let anything keep her from her dreams. This would not be one of the things she could not overcome. Ami, knowing her mother never was much on the caring side. She knew her mother was already out of her comfort zone at her school today and by the look on her face in the car, it would take her some time to recover her dignity and less than sunny disposition she normally had, which consisted of a frowned forehead and somewhat of a stale face for a smile, if that.

As Ami crossed the threshold of the apartment entrance, breathing labored, she grabbed the door to stable herself some. Making her way to the stairs, she reached for the banister, lifted her leg to make the first step. "Ami, Ami!" Rhonda screamed as she dropped everything to the floor. "Ami, baby!" tears begin to stream down her face, as she watched Ami's eyes role back into her head. She dropped down to the floor were Ami had collapsed, "Call, 911!" "Call 911!" screamed Rhonda at the door where she knew Mrs. Johnson was peering. Rhonda knew Ami was all she had, and this situation was about to break her. Her heart raced a mile a minute as she tried to get Ami to respond. She lifted her head into her lap and assured Ami it would be ok.

A few moments later, she heard the chains on the door start to rattle and unlock. As the door continued to rattle, and then finally it opened, "What's wrong with the child suga?" The voice of a Southern Bell emerged from behind her. I have them on the line already, my son gave me this here cellular last year, handy little thing. Lift her arms over her head suga, it will help her breath. Does this child have asthma?" Mrs. Nosey questioned. "She'll be alright, just give her a second." Rhonda, now scared out of her wits, "How did you know, that's what they told me at her school today!" She said as she lifted Ami's arm over her lifeless head and body. "That's it. She's breathin' a little betta, now isn't she?"

"Now you gonna have to calm yourself down and believe God for your child," she said. Rhonda had no idea what she was talking about at this point because she was consumed with the fact that Ami was barely breathing. Rhonda shook her head, yes, and rubbed Ami's forehead. "Suga, I think you need to raise both of her arms and give her a little more support under her head." "Oh, yeah!" Rhonda franticly replied. As Mrs. Johnson hung up the phone with the emergency responders, she walked over to Rhonda again, "Does she have an inhaler at all?" "What is that!" Rhonda replied sharply. "Well, I'm guessing you're going to find out soon enough." Mrs. Johnson said softly.

"When I saw the child coming down the stairs this morning, I could tell she was having an attack, not rocket science to see that suga." "Great," Rhonda thought to herself, "She peeps all day and night, does this lady sleep?" She had never talked to Mrs. Johnson personally, but Ami had once, when she was trying to ask her where her mother was the day she came home from school and Rhonda didn't accompany her, but soon followed with bags in hand about thirty minutes later. Rhonda had warned Ami to be quick about getting in the house and locking the door, but she was stopped for questioning by Mrs. Johnson when things didn't look right. Who was so nosey she had a need to know who came and went every hour of the day? Ms. Nosey was truly her given name, given by all her other neighbors.

"Are you sure they are on their way, maybe I need to just take her? They are taking too long!" Rhonda said, after managing to calm herself down and being careful to follow Mrs. Johnson's instructions as she seemed to know what she was talking about. "What in that tanker you call a car?" Rhonda turned her head quickly and snarled at Mrs. Johnson. "Well, you're doing the best you can, given your situation." Rhonda felt a bit relieved inside and realized Mrs. Johnson was not like anyone she had met besides Mitchell. She was not trying to judge her life based on what she saw, she was just stating the facts. "Well, I guess you're right." Rhonda giggled.

Wow, she thought to herself, it's been a while since someone made her laugh. As painful as it was to admit it, Mrs. Johnson had grabbed a moment of fear and turned it into a connection Rhonda would not soon forget. A few more minutes and suddenly Ami's breathing began to calm even more. "There now. See she is getting better by the minute." Mrs. Johnson said. "Yeah, she does seem to be breathing better now." Rhonda replied. "Ami, baby wake up, honey." Rhonda coached as she rubbed Ami's chest.

"Ami, baby, please wake up." Ami began to open her eyes and with labored breath and begin to speak, "Mommy?" "Yes, baby, I'm right here." Rhonda said. "Now that's a real good sign. Told you Suga. Sometimes you just have to believe God!" said Mrs. Johnson. "I don't really believe in God ma'am." Rhonda replied with a sound of curtness. "Well, I bet you will after this day." Mrs. Johnson said with a knowing in her voice, as a mother knows when a child will understand it all soon.

"What is taking them so long?" Rhonda said in frustration. "Be patient Suga they comin'." replied Mrs. Johnson. They could finally hear the sirens getting closer, and closer. Some of the neighbors entered the hallway as the emergency vehicle parked in front of the building. "Here we go suga, they will be right in," Mrs. Johnson said as she stood watching for them. In rushed three Ambulance workers, rushing over to Ami lying on the floor, as if Rhonda was not sitting under her holding her. "How long has she had asthma?" Rhonda was now feeling a bit neglectful, seeing everyone could see she had asthma, and replied, "It just came on today, at her school." Giving Ami an oxygen mask they loaded her up to place her in the back of the ambulance.

"Don't worry Suga, I will put your bags in my apartment until you come home." "Ok," Rhonda replied to Mrs. Johnson. Climbing into the back of the ambulance, Rhonda began to feel a bit overwhelmed. "Don't worry, Miss. She will be fine in just a little while. I have seen plenty of cases like this and they are usually fine in a few hours." The voice of a busy emergency worker said as she reached for equipment and wrote on her clipboard.

FEELING AGAIN

Now reaching the hospital, Rhonda was surrounded by a lot of medical jargon she did not understand. A lady escorted her to a small desk in the corner, where she told her that everything would be ok with Ami, and that everything that was happening, was normal. For the time being she needed to obtain some information about Ami, directing Rhonda to have a seat in the chair on the other side of her desk. "Who is your insurance through ma'am?" "I am supposed to have it through, I think it's Common Network?" "You don't know for sure?" The lady replied. "No, because I just started my job a while ago, I don't even think its effective yet." Rhonda responded. "Oh, dear, that may be a problem." The young lady said, looking at Rhonda as if she couldn't believe her ears. "Well, let me call them and find out, I believe they can tell me. Let me just get a little more information and we will see." The lady told her.

After some additional questioning and a few calls, the lady found out through Rhonda's insurance company that they had been covered for more than six months, and with a low deductible. "Ms. Hodge, we have all we need, thank you." She called for the attendant to come and escort

Rhonda to the room were Ami was lying in a bed, breathing mask in hand, wide awake. At this point, her hair was all over her head from the rustling and moving that everyone was doing. She looked beautiful to Rhonda, being this was the most afraid she had been of losing her since before she was born.

"Ami, we just keep meeting like this." Rhonda jokingly said. Ami, a bit shocked noticing that her mother was being funny and found it very comforting, as she had felt a bit sad. All of this was happening and seeing her mother's face now full of worry, Ami laughed a little, and Rhonda walked over and grabbed her hand as they waited to see the doctor. As the doctor entered the room, he looked at Ami, then looked at Rhonda, "Hello Ms. Hodge, I'm Dr. Myles Johnson," he said. "Hi," Rhonda said as her eyes lit up at the sight of the man, staring at her as he talked, in a way she had not been looked at in a while.

"Well, it looks like we're dealing with a case of persistent severe Asthma, and from all I have heard from the medical staff about the day, it looks like we may be dealing with a rare case here." "What is that?" "Well, it is a breathing disorder of the lungs, caused by inflammation and from the sound of it Ami may have a type which stems from weakened vessels in the lungs. Could be from birth and just manifesting now or allergens, such as pollen, dust, change in climate. It really just depends." He replied. "Trouble is we have to do some tests to find out what Ami's triggers are, and make sure there is not a more severe underlining condition going on. Then we can take measures to strengthen those vessels and get her in good health." he concluded on the matter. "It's Ami, right," he questioned? "I know, just wanted to make sure you're still with me," he joked. As Rhonda giggled a little. He was rather handsome to her, after all. "No time for that now though," she thought.

"Is she going to be ok, I mean she's not going to die, right?" "No, Ms. Hodge, it is Ms. isn't it" he flirtingly asked? "Yes," Rhonda hesitantly replied. Not knowing what was happening at this point, Rhonda looked down at Ami, seeing she had the widest eyes in the history of eyeballs at that moment. Rhonda now figured that she had better behave before Ami picked up on this flirting that was going on between her and "Dr. Myles". He was rather fine, but that was the least of her concerns at this point.

"Alright, so what do we need to do" she questioned? "Well, we don't need to do a thing but take care of this beautiful little girl at this point. I am going to go and order some tests to ensure this is asthma and hopefully it's just a mild case." He injected, "Once the tests are back, I will prescribe something for her breathing and get you both on your way. If it's not mild, then we may have to go in another direction." he said as he stood to his feet looking down at the computer screen. "I have a list of primary care doctors she can follow up with in a few days," he said as he turned toward the door to leave. "Hang tight and I will return shortly," exiting the room.

"Humm, he will return Mom," Ami said with her eyes side peering at Rhonda, giggling a bit and she laid her head back on the pillow. "Hush girl, you are too grown for your own good!" Rhonda pointed out, realizing Ami was very aware of what was going on between Dr. Myles and her. "Let's just focus on getting you home and out of this stale hospital," she said as she looked around the room frowning. "Didn't seem too stale a moment ago, mom," Ami chuckled. Rhonda laughed as she looked at Ami with her hush smirk. "I'm just hoping this is something that will pass soon," Rhonda said as she walked over and placed her hand on Ami's head. "I just want to get you back to your sweet playful self soon," Rhonda continued. "This has been a ride I don't wish to stay on any longer." Rhonda leaned down to kiss Ami's head, "You gave me such a scare Ami," Rhonda continued, as she heard a knock at the door. "Yes, come in."

"Hi, I'm Michelle, and I will be doing a breathing test on Ami," the young woman said as she blissfully waltzed into the room. "Oh, okay," Rhonda said nervously not noticing she was wringing her hands. Fearful the breathing test would cause Ami to pass out again, she started to wring her hands even more. "Don't worry Ms. Hodge," the nurse said as she looked down at Rhonda's hands. "I'm just going to have her breathe into this tube to check her levels, then we will give her another breathing treatment like she had in the ambulance," she said as she began to place the tubing into Ami's open mouth. "Oh, ok," Rhonda replied with relief. "All of this is rather scary for us," she said in conclusion. "I totally understand. She is just being diagnosed and that alone is scary when you don't know about the illness. She will be just fine, soon," as she reached to move a chair closer to Ami.

"This won't take but a few minutes and then Dr. Myles will be back with her prescription. Hi, sweetie, all of this must be very uncomfortable for you, huh," asked Michelle as she placed the tube a little more into Ami's mouth? "Es," Ami replied, as she clamped her teeth around the tube. Rhonda remembered another time she was in the hospital as she sat in the chair waiting for the doctor to return. As her mind began to recall the events leading up to a long stint in the ICU, she began to clench the arms of the chair she was sitting in.

"Who are you talking to on the phone?" Lacresha turned as she heard a man's voice yell. She shuddered, with a guilty look on her face, remembering the conversation she was just having with the other party as she placed the receiver to the base slowly. "Teresa, you have to help me, I have to get out now. He is on something else, it's not just the drinking now, it's different this time. I'm scared all the time! Teresa, I have to go now, he's back, I will call you soon!" As John entered the room yelling, she could still hear Teresa calling out her name on the line as she placed the phone down. "My sister, baby, she was just checking in on us asking how I was feeling?" "Why, is she checking on how your feeling? What are you telling your family about me," he yelled? Lacresha replied, "Nothing, baby, she just knew I had been a little under the weather and called to see how I was feeling." "Who are you raising your voice to," he questioned, as he

moved closer toward her? "I'm not, John, I'm just tired, is all," she said with a sigh. "What you tired of? Me?" John continued to yell as he walked closer to her, blocking her inside the room. "Is that why you were so quiet on the phone? Who was that, was that the guy you been seeing behind my back? Is that what you're doing, planning on leaving me?" He continued to yell as he grabbed her cheeks and squeezed them together with one hand. "You're not going any...." Bam! Lacresha, feeling herself begin to fall, she also felt a hand in her hair, snatching her head back from a blow to the face from behind. She tried to turn and run away, and she screamed, "Stop John!" She yelled. "Please John!" Umph! As Lacresha's head hit the corner of the table, she felt her body hit the floor and a kick to the back, then to the side. She lay lifeless on the floor, feeling herself slipping in and out of consciousness.

As Lacresha awoke, she could hear people around her. She was feeling extreme pain, as she tried to open her eyes, she soon realized that they were swollen shut. "We may not be able to save the baby, it's in distress and she is fighting for her life." As the days passed into weeks and months, Lacresha remembered waking up to her sister, Teresa, sitting by her side. As she struggled to open her eyes, the light was blinding. She realized she was in the hospital and that she must have been there for months. "Um," as she clears her throat to try and talk, she whispered, "Did he kill me?" "No baby, you're still here, baby," Teresa says softly. "Um," she said softly, struggling to speak. "How long have I been here?" realizing again where she was. "For almost 6 months, you have been in a coma for most of it, because of the swelling." "I'm so glad to see you, baby," said Teresa excitedly. "The b...baby?" Lacresha exclaimed! "Chile she is a fighter too, she is still in there!" Silence fell over the room, as Lacresha began to relax back into the pillow. "Has he been here?" Lacresha asked as fear gripped her. "No, and he better not show his face here," Teresa interrupted!

"The police have been by several times to speak to you. The hospital called to let them know they were going to try and wake you up today. Momma was here, but she had to leave. I know you are glad about that, Chile." Teresa continued to fill Lacresha in on the details. "Chile, we can talk about this later, but Michael and I have some savings and we are going to give it to you so you and the baby can go somewhere safe, start over." Teresa said compassionately. "I can't ask you to do that, this is my mess and I have to fix it," Lacresha said abruptly.

"You're my baby and as long as you have been living, I have been looking out for you and that's not going to stop just because you have seed in your belly, so stop sassing me," she said sternly! "Now let us do this for you and my niece," she said quickly. "Now listen baby, there has been an armed guard outside your door the entire time. Apparently John was being watched long before this and they were building a case against him for heroin and international smuggling of all types. It looks like he is way into this thing more than we could ever know, and that guy he was in business with is nowhere to be found. That may be why he was so different these days." said Teresa.

"He has changed so much. I know he would hit me occasionally, but it was always my fault, I would just make him so mad." "Chile, I know you're not laying up here blaming yourself for this mess. You must want me to put you back under," Teresa said jokingly. "Now you just stop this foolery, there is no reason for a man to put his hands on a woman," Teresa said. "I know. We grew up in all this

disfunction and deception around us as children, but there is a way to come out of that dysfunction and be away from all that mess." Teresa continued, "That man is selfish, greedy and wanted to control you, and that's not love," she said angered yet making sure she wasn't upsetting her sister as she explained the situation at hand!

"Now I know he is your husband, but I'm just gone put the stuff on out there, he's crazy as hell and needs to get got," in her slang talk but with a serious tone. "Listen we can talk about this later, let's just get you well and go from there," Teresa said as she grabbed her hand. "In the meantime, I will do my best to keep the other crazy person from staying for her visits for too long," Teresa said as she laughed. "So they don't have to put you back in a coma or a crazy home, just so you can have some peace." They both laughed and gripped hands.

****

"Good morning Sunshine!" Teresa said as she entered the room for discharge day. "You ready?" "Yes, more than ready!" "Michael is bringing the car around and the nurse said the doctor was on his way with your follow-up instructions," Teresa said as she grabbed the bags from Lacresha's bed and placed them on the cart by the door. Lacresha knew this was going to be an up-hill battle, but she felt it was the only way she would be free from John. "They said it was ok for you to take all of your stuff with you to the safe house once they pick you up later today," Teresa whispered in Lacresha's ear.

"I wonder what name you will have. I will have to get used to calling you by your new name soon, for when they arrange for us to talk." "Yeah, Lacresha will be no more, you will have a new start," Teresa said, quietly. "I'm so afraid all of this will go wrong, I mean, I know *the people he has on his team. What if he finds out I am the lead witness against him? Teresa, if something happens to me, promise me you will take care of my baby, if she makes it here." As the tears begin to roll down their faces, Teresa gets in Lacresha's face leaning down, "Nothing is going to happen to you or this baby do you hear me? Nothing! We got you!" The doctor entered the room with instructions on follow-up care, and the scheduled dates for the remaining physical therapy Lacresha was going to have.*

"Hey Lacresha," a tender male voice spoke, and Lacresha shook to her core. As Lacresha lifted her head sharply to see who was greeting her, she realized it was her brother-in-law, Michael. "Hi, Michael," she struggled to whisper as her voice was not totally recovered from the tubing which had been placed down her throat to keep her breathing while she was in the medically induced coma. "Are you ready, honey," Michael questioned? "Yes," she said as loudly as she could. As they made their way down the hallways to the front entrance, Lacresha paid attention to every person in the hallway, ensuring that John was not lurking somewhere waiting for her to be away from the protective officers who had stood watch outside of her room for the last six months. This was something she had grown accustomed to doing, each time the nurses would make her walk to regain her strength and ensure proper circulation for the sake of the baby.

As she made her way into the back seat of the car, she noticed two unmarked cars sitting near the entrance. She knew they were there not only to ensure her safety, but also discreetly positioned just in case John did show up and try to finish the job he had started. John did not appear and before she knew it, they were off to Teresa and Michael's house where they would meet up with other family members for their final goodbyes. Nervous about facing her mother and her "I told you so's," Lacresha managed to pull herself together to face her mother with confidence. As they arrived at the home, Michael pulled into the garage and closed the door.

"Well, you ready for this, Sis," Teresa asked hesitantly? "Yeah, I guess I have no choice at this point, Lacresha replied with just as much exhaustion in her tone. "You know she is locked and loaded, right?" Teresa giggled and opened her car door with a push. "When is she not?" replied Lacresha. "You already know she is going to explain how you only get one marriage in God's eye's and ask you if you plan on not having sex for the rest of your life, like her." Teresa said with a big chuckle, "But what God don't know won't hurt him, cause her and Mr.!"

"What took y'all so long, we been waiting here for over an hour?" A woman yelled from the garage door leading from the house. "We're carrying precious cargo, we cannot be expected to rush just because you are waiting. You could have always just gone home," Teresa responded, "which would have been a sigh of relief for all of us," Teresa muttered under her breath. "What you say Resa? I know you said something smart?" The woman said from the door. "Y'all get in here, now," she said as she motioned and held the door open. "I'm just trying to figure out when she moved in, cause I don't remember this being her house?" Teresa said under her breath, as she assisted Lacresha from the car. "Chile I can't say which is on my nerves more, your mother or you, and this big belly you have to roll in and out of this car." "Whoa, chile this gone be a big old baby!" "Come on here, the sooner we get you in here, the sooner we can get her out." "You a mess," Lacresha said, as she made her way up the stairs and into the

kitchen of the house.

Come on over here and sit down, Lacresha" a man said from the living room of Teresa's house. "Uncle Thomas, I'm just trying to figure out if you and momma going to pitch in on this here mortgage this next month, cause both of yawl acting like yawl reside here," Teresa teased from the kitchen. "I'm not paying nothing, as long as you my child, your house is mine," her mother said from behind her as she walked into the living room. "Marissa, you can't expect this girl to let you come in here and take over her house, this is a grown woman in here, both grown," Uncle Thomas emphasized. Marissa interjected, "I know they grown, but I'm they…. never mind Thomas, I should of known you would start!" "Hey, Hey," Teresa said quickly. "This evening is not about any of you, this is about saying goodbye to your daughter, your niece and my sister" she said angrily!

As the family moved into the living room to gather and talk, Lacresha knew this was a big decision she was making, but felt it was the only thing she could do to keep her and the baby safe from John. "I am going to miss you all so much, I just can't believe this is happening," Lacresha said as tears began to roll down her face. "I just never thought he would turn out to be such…," as she was interrupted by her mother. "Well, I did! I mean what did you expect? The man came waltzing up to my door, with all of his flash and fluff! I knew from the start he wasn't right. I just want to know what you plan on doing for yourself and this baby now, 'cause I know these people ain't gonna pay your way through life!" Marissa looked Lacresha in the face waiting for her to answer.

"Are you planning on staying single the rest of your life, cause he is still your husband," she said with disdain. "Just stop it, Mom, we all

know where you stand on the one marriage viewpoint, and we ain't buying it," Teresa interrupted. "Lacresha has been through hell these last few months, not to mention what she is facing now and she doesn't need to hear your judging innuendos and foolish talk. You act like everything in your life is so perfect, everyone knows what you think. I mean, how can we not?" Silence fell over the room as Teresa walked from the kitchen. "Not one time did you come to the hospital and ask if she was ok, you just start in on what you think about her life, and mine too, for that matter."

"Now, Teresa, I'm not going to stand for this tone from you. You know I have been busy," Marissa said as she rose from the chair. "Yeah busy doing Mr.," Teresa said, as she was interrupted by Lacresha. "Ok, that's enough guys, I'm just tired and hungry, do I smell food?" "Yeah, if that's what you want to call it, your mother been in the kitchen all day messing up some concoction," Uncle Thomas said with a straight face, to break the mood. "Oh, hush Thomas, you know you gon' eat," Marissa replied. "Let's feed this family, before we say our goodbyes," he said.

TROUBLE ARRIVES

*E*veryone entered the kitchen with somber moods, understanding this could be the last time they would see Lacresha and she knew it. As she sat and tried to eat, she couldn't help but wonder what life would be like for her and her child once she testified against her husband. There were people and things she pretended not to know, about the life he lived. To be honest she was afraid of what he would do to her if she ever left him. Something in her heart knew this was the beginning of an even longer road of fear for her. She struggled to hold back her tears with each bite she took as she and Teresa exchanged subtle smiles and glances at one another throughout the meal. No one really talked too much during dinner. No one really knew what to say or ask for that matter, not even Marissa.

As the hours passed, everyone was lazy from the meal prepared. They sat telling stories Lacresha would not hear again, reflecting on the events which shaped her childhood and teenage years - stories of how Uncle Thomas tortured Marissa as a child and even more so as adults. Memories flooded the room and their hearts as they all came to the realization this would possibly be the last time, they would be able to sit and reminisce together as a complete family unit. As disheartening as this was, they still found a way to express laughter through the tears, especially the tears shed during Uncle Thomas's stories of his childhood shenanigans at Marissa's expense. "Did I ever tell y'all about the time we trapped that skunk and hid it in…."

"Knock, knock, knock," they heard at the door. "Who is it!" Michael said, as everyone turned quickly to look toward the door. "It's not time yet," Teresa asked reluctantly? "No, I don't think so, but they didn't say what time really, Lacresha said." "It's Crystal, a woman said at the door." "Who, Michael asked, as he opened the door." "Hello, my name is Crystal and I'm here to warn you", she said. "May I come in for a minute," she asked nervously? "Uh, yeah," Michael and Teresa replied. "Who are you, Marissa inquired?" "Calm down Marissa and let this little girl talk", Uncle Thomas interjected.

"My name is Crystal ma'am, and I know John, she said softly." "What, now just how you know John? Are you talkin about that no good for nothing?" Marissa yelled as she was interrupted by Thomas. "Now, I'm not going to tell you again, let this girl talk now. What is it child," as he ushered her to come on into the living room? "I just couldn't sit by and let them do this," she said with fear in her eyes. "Do what? Now you are going to have to come on out with it," Teresa said. "John has about twenty men looking for Lacresha all over the city and he gave this as the address they are supposed to hit tonight!" Crystal was wringing her hands, acting as if she was having withdrawals. "They all gonna meet up in two hours and ride by here after everyone goes to sleep. He said he didn't care about the baby or any of you all, he just wanted you dead," she said, as she turned toward Lacresha.

"How did you know to come here, Teresa said?" "I'm risking my life to come here, but I can't have this on me, not no baby and a good

*woman." Everybody tried to tell him you was good, but he on that H
and ain't no talking to him." "He done lost it for real now, this is all
he be talking about, he wrong for this, and I had to come!" Marissa
interrupted, "Yeah he wrong for a lot of stuff." "I got to go," the girl
said as she moved towards the door. "No, you gon' wait right her till
we call the policemen in here," Marissa said, as she grabbed the girl's
arm to stop her." "I can't stay here; they will kill me if they find out I
came here!" "Well you said you was risking your life!" Marissa said
sharply. "Marissa, let that girl go, she did what she was supposed to
do, she told us, now let her go," Thomas yelled!*

*The girl opened the door and walked out, "I'm sorry, you got his baby
in you, that's too much." She said, as she pulled her hood up over her
head and walked down the sidewalk. "Yeah, I just bet," Marissa
said as Michael closed the door and locked it. "Lacresha, where is the
number for the program, we need to call them right now! Teresa said,
as fear swept over everyone in the house, Lacresha pulled the card out
of her purse and with her hands shaking, she handed Teresa the card.
"Here Michael, you call them!" "We have to get out of here!" said
Marissa. "I told you that boy was going to take you down a dark
path, now look at you, got us all in this mess," she said angrily.*

*As the family sat waiting for the police to arrive, a frightening chill
came over the room as if someone had died and the body was sitting in
the room with them. No one knew what these next few minutes would
bring. As Michael headed to the upstairs bedroom, Teresa followed.
"Where you two going?" Marissa questioned. "Now, I done told you
to mind your business Rissa, this is they house and wherever they are
going, it is their business, Leave them to it," Uncle Thomas said.
"Well I don't want to be left here to take they bullets, is all I'm*

saying, I can go home," she said with a smart tone. "Now that is the best darn set of words you have spoken all evening," Thomas exclaimed quickly. "Alright, don't start that up again, we just going to get the guns from the safe," Teresa responded.

"What!" "I can't believe yawl got me in the middle of a shootout. Are those guns registered and do yawl have permits, are you licensed to carry? Heck we'll be in jail with John at this rate," Marissa said with steam rolling from the top of her racoon fir wig. "Your keys are on the table, Marissa, you can leave... at any time," "Hush Thomas," Marissa interrupted, "I just want to know if I'm going to die tonight or be in jail in the morning is all, making her way over to the window to peep from the curtain. "Boom!" Thomas said, as Marissa jumped back from the curtain, grabbing her chest. "Stop it Thomas, you old coon!" Thomas and Lacresha giggled to themselves.

"Well, it's quiet out there, maybe that little girl was just, I don't know," Marissa said as she moved away from the window, ensuring she left a crack so she could continue to view anything moving outside, besides a dog. "How long does it take for them to get here? Michael called over forty-five minutes ago." Marissa questioned, as she moved the blinds apart just a little more. "Mom, get out of the curtain and blinds, I couldn't take it if something happened to any of you!" Lacresha said as she moved towards her mother, grabbing the curtains to close them and slightly pushing her mother away. "Well, that is nice of you to say, seeing you the one that got us into this awful mess in the first place," her mother responded sharply.

Just then they saw red and blue lights flashing into the house. Everything in the room was now standing completely still as though time and life had come to an abrupt halt. "Teresa," Marissa yelled *from the living room. "They here!" Teresa and Michael were already coming down the stairs, Teresa had a look on her face of pain. She and Lacresha had always been so close, she did not know how to not be the mother in her life. For a time, she was the mother because Marissa struggled so with anxiety and depression from her divorce. She had basically closed herself away for many years in her bedroom when they were younger. Only to come out and tell them what was wrong with the house, then quickly retreat to her "devils' den," which is what they would call it in secret.*

"I don't know how to do this? How can I," Lacresha paused, as tears began to roll down her face? Uncle Thomas grabbed her as her body went limp in his arms, "Come on now here, long as I have known you, I have never known you to be of weak constitution. You gonna do this, for you and that great nephew or niece of mine, and you gonna get the chance to live and live safe and free from this foolishness." Thomas said as he lifted her face toward his.

"Now listen, everyone makes choices in relationships that don't always bring them to the place they thought or saw when they added that person to their puzzle. You know how to take the pieces of the puzzle that don't fit away and continue to try other pieces. Before you know it, you have a beautiful picture staring at you. This is just the piece that don't fit, but the puzzle didn't change, baby girl. And it's still going to be beautiful if you keep working it, ok, adding the right pieces as you go. Right now, is the going part, so gather yourself and go and make a new life for you and that baby. You will find your way soon enough, just find your way," he said, as tears filled his eyes and he held her as tight as he could.

Lacresha lifted herself up, looked around the room and she found everyone in the room had been moved to tears, even Marissa. Even though she still had her angry stare piercing the side of Thomas's head. "Marissa, I think your ice is melting," Thomas said, with a chuckle. "What ice, Thomas? I ain't even drinking nothing." "The ice over your heart, Thomas said, breaking the emotional mood, as everyone laughed historically. "Now come on here and let's get your things," Uncle Thomas said as he helped Lacresha to her feet. "Michael go on now, go let those officers in, so we can get the final details and say our goodbye's," he said.

As Michael moved towards the door, they began to hear tires screeching outside and a loud burst of sirens, as they all rushed to the door to see what the commotion was. Lucrecia yells, "That's him." Her voice barely a dull roar, yet, Thomas stood by grabbing her hand. "Now just don't you worry now, we got you and the policeman is here." Marissa agreed with him quickly, "Yes, that's right, that's right!" Everyone turned their heads quickly and looked at Marissa with their mouth's half open in disbelief. "Now just hush, I care, no matter what yawl say, I care!" "Now get out of my face," Marissa yelled.

REALITY CHECK

Miss Hodge, Rhonda" a voice echoed twice, "we would like to admit Ami and run a few more tests, but I think we are almost out of the woods. Her breathing seems to be somewhat stable for now, but we want to just watch her and make sure the meds we are giving her will continue to open her air ways." Michelle turned to Ami and said, "You want to hang out with us for a while, don't you? I promise we will make this as fun as possible for someone in your predicament, ok?" Ami shook her head yes and looked over at her mom, as if to say she was sorry, but also realizing this meant they would be spending extra money so she wasn't getting that bike she had hinted about all year for her birthday, too.

Dr. Johnson entered the room, "Well young lady, seems we are going to have to get you to stay around for a bit, some of your lab test didn't show the results I had hoped for. That's not too bad is it?" "We are pretty nice, huh? I sure would love to have you around for a day or so." He expressed as his eyes cut over to Rhonda, as to ensure she knew he was also referring to her. Rhonda shuddered at the thought, at this point all she could think about was James and all she had been through to stay safe. Staying away from the opposite sex, she wasn't about to jeopardize Ami and her safety now, not even if he was fine as all get out. "However, I will not be your doctor on the floor where you will be staying, he said, picking up on the disinterested vibe Rhonda was now giving off. "Well, I have to call my manager and make sure my shifts are covered for a couple of days, but it should be fine as long as she needs to stay," Rhonda said, in a questioning tone.

Dr. Johnson could tell something had changed from before. Rhonda was no longer giving him the vibe he once felt. "Yes, this is necessary to ensure her safety on this particular medication. Also, we found some very weak vessels in the core of her lungs. We want to start her on some other medications which will help to strengthen those areas. From the tests we ran, she is a little more advanced than we had originally thought and given this is a rare type of asthma we don't want to take any chances. I am just glad we caught it at this age and stage," he responded with a disappointed tone.

"If you would just continue to be patient with us while we put all the puzzle pieces together, we will ensure that we have a beautiful picture staring back at us," he said as he turned to exit the room. Rhonda, looked as though she had just had the scare of her life and quickly turned to look at the doctor as he finished his sentence. She could not believe he said those words. The words Uncle Thomas told "Lacresha" before she was whisked away into her new life as "Rhonda". This time was the turn of events in her life with Ami getting ill. Those words seemed to reach into her soul and shake her to her core. She didn't know if it was a good shake or a bad one at this point, and she wasn't interested in finding out.

As the doctor turned and looked at Rhonda, he began to wonder why her demeanor had changed. Then he said with hesitancy, as he stood at the door, "I would like to call and follow up with Ami in a few days, after she has released to return home." Rhonda couldn't help gazing into his mocha colored, hazel eyes with an almost excitement about her. He was a tall chocolate sip of coffee and she couldn't help herself. "Well I think that would be ok, as long as it's Ami you're interested in following up on." Now, he knew for sure she and he were putting out vibes and yet he didn't understand what changed so suddenly. However, he knew he would eventually find out.

With a stutter in his voice, he chuckled a little and said, "Yes, why else would I call? Please have Ami follow up with her primary care as soon as possible, once released. We want to stay on top of this as much as possible." Dr. Myles picked up his papers and moved toward the computer by the door. "I am going to go ahead and prescribe a breathing machine just as the one we have here and the nurse will come in and show you how to use it. She will have to do this at least three times a day, until we get her breathing under control." Dr. Myles sat down on the stool in front of the computer and started to type.

"The nurse kind of already came in and showed us, but I'm sure another lesson would be fine." Rhonda said as she was unable to help staring at him as he sat typing. "Ok then, I'll let her know. It was nice meeting you and as I said before, I will follow up in a few days," he said with a grin winking at Ami as he stood. "Auhh, but you don't have my number." Rhonda quickly responded as to ensure she gave it to him. "Oh, it's in the chart," he replied closing the door. As he left the room, Ami looked at her mother with a kiddush grin, "You know you like him." "Hush Ami, I'm not worried about no man, I'm worried about you right now, and you're all that matters."

As the moments went by, a nurse came in with a breathing machine, "Hi, my name is Kendra and I'm here to show you how to use this breathing machine." She hurriedly sat it on the stand, by the table which was closer to Ami. "The doctor will call a prescription in for a breathing machine and the formula that goes into the machine before Ami is released." "Ok, thank you," Rhonda said nervously, as she looked at the machine. The nurse explained how the machine worked again and what it did for Ami, how it would open her lungs and allow any congestion to surface, Rhonda felt relief. This was something she could handle.

As the nurse finished the treatment demonstration and left the room, Rhonda realized how much time had passed, between them taking Ami for tests and coming in and out of her room, she remembered her phone had been dead for hours. She realized she needed to make a phone call or two.

To be honest she just needed to take a moment to breathe all of this in and clear her thoughts.

Rhonda just wanted to wash away the memories which had just flooded her heart and mind. To be honest, all she really wanted to do was see and talk to Teresa, but she knew she wasn't supposed to reach out in any way. "Ami honey, I have to go and make a phone call. I will let the nurse know I am stepping out, so they can keep an eye on you." Rhonda, turned to walk toward the door, "You ok?" "Yeah, I'm ok," Ami replied, as she tried to sit up in the bed and grabbed the remote for the television. "Ok, I will be back soon, I won't be long." "Ok," Ami replied again.

Rhonda opened the door and walked over to the nurse's station. "Excuse me, where can I find a private phone?" Rhonda asked a young woman sitting behind the desk with her head planted in a book. "I'm sorry, what, what you say?' The young woman replied, as she slowly leaned in Rhonda's direction, as if she did not want to turn from her book. "I'm sorry, I was asking for a private phone, I need to make a call?" "Oh, I'm sorry, my book was getting good," the young lady responded with excitement in her voice. "Just down this hall and to your left, should see it sitting in a small conference room on the table," she explained.

"Oh, can you keep an eye out for my daughter or ask someone to, until you get past the good part of your book and are able to pay attention?" Rhonda said sarcastically. "Oh, honey I'm not new to this, I'm true to this, I am watching my rooms, but I will even watch your daughters, even though she is not in one of my rooms," the woman said back sarcastically. "I will even go and explain the call light system to her real quick, so she knows what to do if she needs anything from her nurse, while you are gone."

Rhonda, rolling her eyes and smiling as she turned to walk away, realized that she liked this young woman very much. As she entered the conference room, the only thought on her mind was making sure she had coverage for the next few days. As she picked up the phone to dial, she remembered the words of Teresa the last time they saw each other. *"Lacresha as long as I'm alive I will never change my number. I will always leave word for you to find us if we have to move, you know the spot."*

As the memory continued to play in her head, she started to dial the number and before she could speak, she heard a familiar voice on the other line, "Hello." The voice, brought tears to her eyes, "Hello? Who's calling please," as silence gripped the line. Rhonda began to whimper through her tears, trying to be quiet and just hear the voice on the other end. "I know someone is there, I can hear you breathing," the voice said on the other line.

"Who is this, is something wrong with your mouth," the voice questions. The woman realizing the person on the other end of the phone was weeping said suddenly, "Lacresha, baby is that you?" The woman at the other end began to question. "It's me, baby, just say something, just." As the phone line disconnected. Rhonda knew she had miss dialed her work number because her heart was in her fingers. She picked up the phone once again trying to gather her composure and watched her fingers hit each number, ensuring, she did not miss a digit. "Hi, this is Rhonda Hodge; can I talk to Sam?" "Hol' on," a woman sad, as the phone slammed down. "Carrie, tell Sam, telephone."

Moments passed and a man's voice deep and heavy on the other end, "Yes, *Exclusive*, may I help you," he questioned. "Hey, Sam this is Rhonda. My daughter is real sick, and I need a couple of days off." "You're a manager and I need you to find somebody to watch your kid, I need you on your shifts," the man said with an angry tone. Rhonda replied, "I can't, they have admitted her in the hospital, and she won't get out for a couple days." Sam, calming his voice said, "Oh, well why you didn't say that first, then. I will see if I can get somebody in here, let me work it out. You been real good about comin' in here on your off days and you really hold this place down, I can give you this for sure. Don't worry 'bout it, just get the kid well," he said as he cleared his throat. "Just let me know if you need more time, I got you."

Rhonda could hear concern in Sam's voice for the first time since she started working there. She knew he liked her, no matter how hard he tried to prove to her he didn't like anybody who worked for him. It was his business, and the success of his restaurant was all he was concerned about. "Ok, I will," she said, as she sniffed knowing he could tell she had been crying. Sam knew Rhonda was not the type to cry, especially not since he had spent the last six months testing that theory, so this had to be serious. "You need anything?" Sam asked hesitantantly, as to not show too much concern or let on that he actually cared. "No, Sam, but thank you for asking," Rhonda said as she reached for a tissue from a box sitting on the table by the phone. "Ok, I got you," Sam said as he hung up the phone. Rhonda could not believe he responded so kindly, well kindly for Sam that is.

As she sat in the chair for a moment, she thought about the voice on the other end of the phone. Wishing she would have had the courage to speak and just say she was ok, or could call again to hear the voice once more. She knew it was evident that she was ok, and she wouldn't dare call again. Rhonda could not figure out how she had dialed the number involuntarily, as though her fingers had a mind of their own. To hear her on the phone only made her want to know how everyone was doing, wishing she had a normal life which included her family. It was weird not knowing where John was or if he was still in jail or not.

As she sat remembering the trial, the days which lead up to it, she could not help but remember the young woman and how she saved her family on that long night. "Woman Found Dead in Alley Dumpster," the title of the article read, "Has been identified as Crystal Simmons. She was a known gang member with the gang organization of John Davis, the notorious drug boss and international leader of a crime syndicate who is currently on trial for trafficking heroine and chemical warfare arms, officials are still searching for suspects and one of the ringleaders of this syndicate." She remembered the article word for word, as it had been etched in her brain. Rhonda knew this girl had truly risked her life to save her and her child. She could not help but hurt inside thinking of the torture this girl had to have gone through before they took her life. Although the timeline of her death did clear John from any physical involvement, she knew it was done for him, or because of him, by his crew.

Shaking herself from her memories, Rhonda realized she had been gone for quite some time and needed to find her way back to Ami. She wasn't the best with directions at this point, so she tried to follow the lady's instructions backwards this time. Managing to make her way back to Ami's room, a young man and older woman came into the room and headed towards Ami's bed, grabbing the rails positioned to the side and below the bed, pulling them up and locking them. "Hi, I'm Steve and this is Marissa, we will be escorting Ami to her room on the 4th floor." "Oh, I wondered who you where and what you were doing, you all moved so fast," Rhonda said sarcastically. "Well we just have a lot to do, and most times patients have been waiting so long they are a little frustrated by the time we get to them. We don't want to keep them waiting for too long," he said hurriedly.

FACING THE DARKNESS

As they entered the hospital room, it was as though they had entered an amusement park. Rhonda and Ami both looking around the room, saw that the bed they would place her in had a slide to exit and stair steps to step down on. The bed was made to look like a treehouse with a lace cover hanging down, as if to accommodate a princess. Ami, excited to see the room with all the books, toys and games surrounding it, smiled as if her face would break. Rhonda realized she was in another glorified situation and this time there was no escaping, at least not for the next few days.

Over the next several days Rhonda and Ami felt as though they were on a mini vacation, aside from the tests and the late night and early morning breathing treatments. They could not remember the last time they had this much fun. Rhonda didn't leave Ami's side very much and when she did it wasn't for long. The staff and the doctors treated them like royalty. Rhonda had not realized that this was because Dr. Myles had been up to visit Ami every day. Each day he left a vase with two roses of different colors, one for Ami and one for her mother, paying a nurse to inform him when Rhonda was away from the room and swearing Ami to secrecy.

"Mommy, our roses are here," Ami would inform her mother each day. Rhonda looked at Ami, often thinking to herself, "What was so special about the roses each day?" She had not realized they meant something very special to Ami. The entire hospital knew it had to be something special about this family for Dr. Myles to take the time to personally check on Ami. They soon started to understand that he was correct, there was a special love and care Rhonda had toward Ami and the staff. Each day Dr. Myles would inquire how the mother was holding up - after he inquired about Ami, of course. Dr. Myles was a man who had excellent morals, he was distinguished and just down right gorgeous. He didn't seem to know how fine he was, his humility was one of his greatest attractions, very wise and selfless. He took no interest in things which did not reflect what he stood for and the entire hospital knew and respected him greatly for it.

Ami was adjusting to the medication nicely and the day came for them to leave the hospital. You would have thought they were part of a large family and were leaving for a long trip. All the staff came into Ami's room with well wishes and lots of stuffed animals to send them off. Rhonda had never experienced this type of treatment and was a little uncomfortable. But because Ami was so happy, she smiled and allowed Ami to be lavished with the gifts.

As they left the hospital, Rhonda couldn't help but wonder why all of this was happening. She remembered her mother telling her, "God has a plan in everything," but she didn't know her Mother's God and was as far away from Him as she felt her mother was at the time. Finally, getting Ami settled in for bed after her breathing treatment, she kissed her good night and told her to call her if she needed her. "I'm tired too honey, this has been an exhausting time for us, huh?"

After laying down for about two hours, she heard a cry "Mommy!" "Mommy!" "I can't breathe!" Rhonda leaped from her bed and rushed to Ami's room. "Ami, are you OK?" She asked. "No, my chest feels heavy," Ami replied, with a groggy tone in her voice. Rhonda reached for the breathing machine and opened the lid to pour in the solution. "This should help you honey. Mommy is going to take good care of you now. Here you go, that's it," as she placed the mask over her face, according to the previous instructions by the nurse.

As Ami dozed back off to sleep, Rhonda sat and waited for the medicine to run out. She removed the mask slowly from around Ami's head and placed it beside her on the nightstand. Then she turned the machine off and left, leaving the door slightly cracked. She returned to her bedroom for just a few more hours of sleep before she would have to do it all over again.

The next morning, Rhonda woke a bit early (because her body had gotten used to being up at zero dark thirty). She took a few minutes to shower and decided that she needed to call Michelle to let her know of the past few days events and that she would not be coming to work. She still could not believe it was okay with their boss. She told Michelle of their conversation, and how she could not believe he was so understanding, Michelle jokingly replied, "Well that's because you're fine and he would love to take you out." "Girl ain't nobody thinking about that man!" Rhonda said with shock. "Chile, I don't mess where I eat, so he can forget it!" she said as she giggled.

"Well, all I know is, he's not that nice on any day to any of us, I'm just sayin'," Michelle said, with a smile in her voice. "Alright girl, I'll talk to you later," Rhonda replied as to cut the conversation short on the subject. As Rhonda hung up the phone and went in to check on Ami, she realized she had missed her normal day of grocery shopping for the week and she still needed to get the groceries she left with Mrs. Nosey.

She entered Ami's room and found her wide awake sitting up in the bed drawing. Ami was used to waking up at zero dark thirty, too. "Good morning, my love," Rhonda said with a smile. She felt that the worst of this situation was behind them now since Ami was not looking as drained as the previous days. "I need to run to the store honey. Do you want to stay here, or come with me?" "I think I'm ok to stay here," Ami said, with an I'm ok in her voice. "Ok, well I'm gonna ask Mrs. Nosey if she will keep an eye on you until I get back. I shouldn't be but a few minutes," she said, as she turned toward the door of the room and grabbed her purse and her keys from the table.

Rhonda headed downstairs and knocked on Mrs. Nosey's

door, "Hi, it's Rhonda, from upstairs. I was wondering if you could do me a favor?" As the door unlatched about five locks, and a little framed woman opens the door, fully dressed, well put together, Rhonda thought to herself, "This lady is jazzy!" Mrs. Johnson opened the door with a sweet smile and questioned, "Yes dear, how can I help and how is your daughter?" "She's better, just resting," Rhonda replied. "Turns out she has asthma," Rhonda said with re-assurance. "Well I could've told you that," Mrs. Nosey said sarcastically. "Yeah I figured," Rhonda said sarcastically in return. She knew the real Mrs. Nosey would stand up at some point during the encounter.

"I was wondering if you could keep an eye on her, while I run to the store for a few things?" Rhonda said with hesitation in her question. "Sure, I can do that, do you need to give her my phone number?" She questioned. "No, but if you just keep an eye out, she knows to get you if something goes wrong. She should be fine, but I just want to make sure somebody is watching out for her," Rhonda said looking towards the exit. "Honey I've been watching out for you all from day one and I'll be here," she said with a giggle in her voice. "Stop back by when you put your groceries up, I got something for you. And don't worry about your daughter, she's going to be fine, honey. God knows that child is strong, and she can handle this," said Mrs. Nosey with assurance." "Yeah...yeah, but I'm not so sure I can." Rhonda said as she turned to leave. "Oh yes you can," Mrs. Nosey said, as Rhonda hurriedly rushed to her car.

Tears began to run down her face, as she sat down in the car, she couldn't understand why this was happening. Thinking to herself, after all she had been through to have Ami, she was not about to let some late stage onset of asthma take her away. Finally, reaching the store front, she sat in the car for a few more moments while she composed herself. The last thing she needed was for someone to look at her crazy. She checked her attitude and makeup in the mirror of her car, which was barely hanging on to the metal hinge. She closed it, then pushed it up, grabbed her purse and made her way into the store.

As she walked down the aisles at the grocery store, she couldn't help but remember the day she told James she was pregnant. They had met in college and married early after graduation. He was a tall sip of chocolate milk back then, and she fell hard for him and his goals. Rhonda had her degree in business and James had a degree in chemistry minoring in international business economics, of all things. Says a lot for how things turned out, she thought to herself. James was so excited. The next day he went out and bought a gold locket inscribed with "Daddy's Forever," inside. As she remembered him lifting the picture and showing her the inscription, she began to remember the promises he made. She did not know how everything went so wrong.

James was a sweet man who got hooked up with a shady business partner that lead him down a path of money and glory, which was short-lived. James always talked about the international trade market and how smart Mark was. After the first two years, James stopped talking and she knew he was changing right before her eyes. He no longer called her in the middle of the day to check on her and her day, he started missing family events and always had some excuse that didn't make sense.

Soon he started drinking heavily and telling her she didn't have anything to do with his business life, she was his wife and that was the role she played. His business partner was killed after three years, the body was never recovered. Rhonda always felt something was missing from the story, but James never wanted to talk about it. James took over the business although Rhonda didn't know what the business was exactly anymore, people and things started to change and before she knew it James was surrounded by people she wasn't allowed to know. She soon learned everything about James was all wrong.

He started to call her names, using words she had never heard from him, coming in smelling like he had been in the bar all night with someone other than her on his clothes. At first, she thought, he had become dependent on the alcohol but soon found out he was doing a lot more than alcohol. The calls started coming later and later in the night, and from his tone something was always going wrong on the other end. Rhonda knew in her heart things with James had gotten shady. He began to beat her and treat her as if she was his property, keeping her away from anyone he felt could influence her to leave him.

After the first time, she remembered that he promised

never to do it again and that he would always take care of her. The beatings started to happen more often and the apologies less and less. It had become her fault because she always questioned him. When she told him she was pregnant he promised to change and take care of her and his child. But later she discovered there was a lot more going on with James then she knew. She would pick up his phone and answer it and a woman would be on the other line. Each time her voice sounded different, as if there were many different women.

He would tell her it was a client or someone else's girlfriend but something in her knew better. As she continued down the aisles, she told herself that was her past and it wasn't worth dwelling on now. She had a new life with Ami, and she intended to protect her and keep her safe. As she checked out from the grocery store, she started to wonder what Mrs. Nosey meant when she said, "God knew Ami was strong."

Opening the door to her apartment, she placed the groceries on the table and went in to check on Ami. She saw that she was sleeping so she walked over to check her breathing, making sure she was ok. "Ami honey, I'm home. I'm going to make you something to eat, but you go ahead and rest." She put the groceries away and went downstairs to Mrs. Nosey's place. Remembering she said she had something to give her, Rhonda wondered what it was. Plus, she needed to grab her bags she had from days ago. "I sure hope this lady ain't Jehovah's witness, that's all I need."

She knocked on the door, and about five locks later, Mrs. Nosey opened the door and looked through a crack in the door, "Oh you made it back. Here come on in," she said invitingly as if they had been friends for a long time. Rhonda stepped inside and to her surprise Mrs. Nosey 's apartment fit the way that she was dressed. The apartment was an elaborate layer full of expensive furniture and trinkets; no real pictures around, just a lot of nice things.

"I love your home." "Oh, thank you dear, I kinda like it too!" She handed Rhonda a small box with some books in it, along with her grocery bags. Pulling out a black book and pointing to it, she said with excitement, "Now this book is the most important one in the box. There's a concordance in the front for passages you can read to Ami every day or night." Now make sure you read it to her and if you feel like it, read some for yourself. You look like you could use a Good Word," she said smartly.

There she was, Mrs. Sassy, Rhonda thought as she said, "Thank you." "You're welcome. Let me know if you need anything." "Come to think of it, I haven't seen you with a man around here. Maybe one day you would like to meet my son? He sure is a tall drink of water. You know, his daddy was a tall drink of water too, God rest his soul." Mrs. Johnson said with a hint of lust. "Them pearly whites, baby, had me swimming in the head!" She shouted. "Auhhh... no I think, I'm, ok. I'll just take the books for now," Rhonda said, as she turned towards the front door and started to walk. She was trying to get out the door as fast as she could, thinking to herself, "If he is as crazy as this lady, I sure don't want to meet him." "Well let me know if you change your mind," she yelled as Rhonda started to close the door. "He's a hot young one, if I do say so myself" she said, voice elevated with excitement.

YOU'RE INVITED

As Rhonda perused through all the books, she found books with titles like, "Overcoming Past Hurts," "Finding the Courage to Love Again," "Encounters with God," and "Moments of Stillness." She thought to herself, "Well she may have well been a Jehovah's witness with all these holy self-help trilogies she gave me," giggling to herself.

She pulled the black book out of the box and laid it on the table. As she put the groceries away that she had retrieved from Mrs. Nosey. She picked up the black book that Mrs. Nosey was so excited about. The front cover said, *The Message*. She wondered what the message was. She made herself a cup of tea and retreated to her room for a few moments of quiet. As she looked in the front of the book, she saw a long list, alphabetically ordered, of different issues. Such issues, like "anger backslidden" and a lot of other things like "forgiveness" "envy" and other things she had no idea about until she got to "healing". She decided to take a look at the first passage listed.

She turned the pages to find Matthew 15:21-28 MSG

[21-22] From there Jesus took a trip to Tyre and Sidon. They had hardly arrived when a Canaanite woman came down from the hills and pleaded, "Mercy, Master, Son of David! My

daughter is cruelly afflicted by an evil spirit." [23] Jesus ignored her. The disciples came and complained, "Now she's bothering us. Would you please take care of her? She's driving us crazy." [24] Jesus refused, telling them, "I've got my hands full dealing with the lost sheep of Israel." [25] Then the woman came back to Jesus, went to her knees, and begged. "Master, help me." [26] He said, "It's not right to take bread out of children's mouths and throw it to dogs." [27] She was quick: "You're right, Master, but beggar dogs do get scraps from the master's table." [28] Jesus gave in. "Oh, woman, your faith is something else. What you want is what you get!" Right then her daughter became well.

She wondered what those words meant, thinking to herself, "I can't believe He called her and her daughter dogs," "Wait how did He know her daughter was healed? Can Ami be healed like that?" She started to question. She didn't understand, but something in her knew she would find out if she kept reading.

Rhonda, now completely engulfed in the message, realizing she was reading another form of the Bible, went back to the front of the book and looked for other words she thought would bring her clarity. As Rhonda skimmed through the many passages, she noticed there was one set named John, thinking to herself, there couldn't possibly be anything good in this one with the name John. She decided to look and see just what it was about.

John 1:1-18 MSG

> [1-2] The Word was first, the Word present to God, God present to the Word. The Word was God, in readiness for

God from day one. [3-5] Everything was created through him; nothing-not one thing!- came into being without him. What came into existence was Life, and the Life was Light to live by. The Life-Light blazed out of the darkness; the darkness couldn't put it out. [6-8] There once was a man, his name John, sent by God to point out the way to the Life-Light. He came to show everyone where to look, who to believe in. John was not himself the Light; he was there to show the way to the Light. [9-13] The Life-Light was the real thing: Every person entering Life he brings into Light. He was in the world, the world was there through him, and yet the world didn't even notice. He came to his own people, but they didn't want him. But whoever did want him, who believed he was who he claimed and would do what he said, He made to be their true selves, their child-of-God selves. These are the God-begotten, not blood-begotten, not flesh-begotten, not sex-begotten.

Somehow, Rhonda felt the words start to speak to her. She had heard the story of Jesus from her mother many years before, yet she never really thought about it. She remembered her mother always saying, "Jesus is the light of the world and whenever you feel alone remember He is always there; He was and will always be."

Although she never really thought about it, she really didn't listen to her mother, then. Reading these words now were almost like pieces to a puzzle she had never solved, and she wanted to know more.

[14] The Word became flesh and blood and moved into the neighborhood. We saw the glory with our own eyes, the one-of-a-kind glory, like Father, like Son, Generous inside and out, true from start to finish. [15] John pointed him out and

called, "This is the One! The One I told you was coming after me but in fact was ahead of me. He has always been ahead of me, has always had the first word." [16-18] We all live off his generous bounty, gift after gift after gift. We got the basics from Moses, and then this exuberant giving and receiving, this endless knowing and understanding- all this came through Jesus, the Messiah. No one has ever seen God, not so much as a glimpse. This one-of-a-kind God-Expression, who exists at the very heart of the Father, has made him plain as day.

After reading this, it was as if a clear picture was being revealed to her of a man, or God, Himself being placed in the body of a baby and coming to earth. She began to think about the Christmas story her mother would read to Teresa and her as a child. "The baby being wrapped in clothing and lying in a manger. This was the lamb, like in the old testament, when they used to kill the lambs and other animals. Why would God place Himself in this position? Why would He want to save us and what was salvation?" she thought. All the talk her mother used to do was now playing in her head and she was overwhelmed by all of it.

"Well, it definitely, isn't about the John I know. He was darkness and would never lead anyone to light. She sat for a few more moments thinking about what she had read, wondering if she really understood what she read. She needed more and she knew this book was not going to explain itself to her. She needed answers and there was only one person who she knew could give them. Suddenly, she heard a call of, "Mommy, are you here?" Ami was awake and emerged from the shadows of the hallway. "Yes, baby

I'm here, in the living room," Rhonda responded. "How did you sleep?" she asked. "Ok, I guess. I'm feeling better now," Ami said, with a smile. "Good, baby. I knew that rest would do you good."

Weeks passed and Rhonda spent most of her evenings sitting in a rocking chair reading *The Message* to Ami. Ami would often fall asleep but Rhonda, being so taken by the stories and the way they were written, could not seem to put the book down. There was a passion birthing in her, and she just could not seem to get enough. After reading for a few hours, she would always make it a point to leave the book there, in the chair, on top of her blanket she used to snuggle with, knowing if she took the book back to her room, she would find ways to continue reading and get very little sleep.

She wanted to know more about this Jesus and who he was. Could *The Message* be what she had been missing this whole time? The answer was still not clear, she decided to herself. She was going to have to spend some time with the one person she knew could give her the answers she was looking for, or at the least, point her in the right direction. Yes, she would have to spend some quality time with Mrs. Nosey, and she shuddered at the thought.

The weeks had passed so quickly, Rhonda did not know the last time she felt this rested. Monday morning was approaching, and Ami was anxious to return to school, although Rhonda made sure she kept up with her schoolwork. It felt like forever for the two of them and they both were ready to get back to their normal. This had been a much needed rest for Rhonda, even though, the stress of Ami's condition still weighed heavily on her. Her biggest worry was whether she would get a call, especially from the school at some point, telling her Ami was sick again.

It was Sunday afternoon and Rhonda settled within herself this was her last evening of being home with Ami and her mini vacation and she wasn't going to let her fears ruin it. She was going to do what she had read in *The Message* and trust in this God she had read about, and not lean to her understanding. Even though she knew her understanding was limited.

As Rhonda prepared an early dinner, which she had not been able to do in a long time, she thought about Mrs. Nosey and when she would get the time to talk with her about this Jesus she was reading about. Finally, dinner was ready, just a few final touches and Ami and she could sit for dinner. While Ami and she set the table, there was a knock at the door. Ami and Rhonda both looked at each other knowing neither of us were expecting anyone. Rhonda motioned for Ami to retreat to her room and lock the door, as this was the routine whenever someone knocked unexpected until Rhonda could see who it was.

"Hello, it's Mrs. Johnson from downstairs," a voice said from behind the door. "I was wondering what smelled so good this early in the day," she said. Rhonda unlocked the door and opened it a bit, taken aback. "Hello Mrs. Johnson, how are you?" Rhonda greeted. "Ami, honey you ready for dinner?" she yelled as she invited Mrs. Johnson in. "Honey you got these hallways stankin', I'm surprised the dogs ain't howlin", she said, as she stepped into the apartment looking around. "I'm just back from service and thought I would stop by and check on you two and invite myself for a plate of whatever you were cooking."

"I made this sock-it-to-me cake yesterday and thought you two might want a piece," she said as she extended her arms. "I made it for my son but he's always so busy, I know it will just sit and go to waste if I don't share. What in the world is that delicious smell coming from these walls honey?" Mrs. Johnson asked as she raised her head and smelled around in the air. "I'm sorry if I'm imposing but I just knew you wasn't going to come down and invite me, as my mother always said, God Rest her soul, A closed mouth don't get fed!" As Mrs. Nosey finished her hurried speaking Rhonda couldn't help but feel a little overwhelmed, but something in her was smiling.

Mrs. Nosey was the first person in the building to ever take an interest in her and Ami. She had to admit, even though this was the sassiest person she had met since she and Ami had moved to this city, she was really starting to grow on her. Plus, she reminded her of her family. Rhonda with a smile on her face, turned and looked at Ami with an unsure grin, "Well we are having, collard greens with turkey, black eyed peas, with ox tails and gravy, and corn muffins." "Now, I hope you didn't make them old box muffins. I hope you put a little effort into some scratch ones?" Mrs. Johnson inquired. "Yes Ma'am, would you care to join us?" Rhonda said. "Well I don't mind if I do, I was wondering when you were gonna ask." Mrs. Johnson said with a smile.

"Where can I sit this sock-it-to-me?" she questioned, as she walked towards the kitchen. Rhonda, looking at Ami who had the biggest grin on her face, shrugged her shoulders as if to say she didn't know what else to do at this point. Rhonda walked behind Mrs. Nosey and directed her to an open space on the counter in the kitchen. "Chile that sock-it-to-me gets heavy after a while," Mrs. Johnson said as she placed the cake on the counter. "Ami, Baby, set another place at the table." Rhonda directed. Ami began to set another setting, grabbed a glass from the cabinet and placed it above the plate she had placed on the table. "Now you're sure I'm not imposing?" Mrs. Johnson asked, as she chuckled a bit before sitting down in her spot.

"No Ma'am, it's been a while since we had anyone over for dinner," Rhonda replied. "Try almost never," Ami said sarcastically. "You know, I was just about to say that!" Mrs. Johnson said with a laugh. "Well that's because we really don't know a lot of people right now, and I work a lot, so I don't have a lot of time," Rhonda said in her defense. "Well, honey, this life you are living isn't going to live itself. You have to find time to work and play, can't be about business all the time," replied Mrs. Nosey. "We are here to have an abundant life, one full of experiences, love, glory and faith!" Mrs. Nosey said as she continued to position her chair. "Now come on here and let's see what you workin' with these oxtails," she said as she pulled her chair closer to the table. Rhonda giggled and thought to herself, "Mrs. Nosey is wise for a smart aleck."

Opening the dish of oxtails, Rhonda began to serve herself and the two of them joined in. "I tell you this looks and smells wonderful! They don't cook like this around here. What part of the south you from, dear?" Mrs. Johnson inquired. "From what I'm tasting you from the Deep South, like Louisiana or Texas," she added. Rhonda, thought to herself, "How did she know that?" Rhonda quickly changed the subject. "We have been reading the book you gave us, *The Message*. I've been wanting to stop by and talk to you about it but with Ami recovering I didn't have time." Rhonda said hoping Mrs. Nosey wouldn't catch on.

"Well I'm here now, what did you want to know" Mrs. Nosey asked with excitement? *The Message* talks about healing is even for the dogs," Rhonda said with a bit of an attitude. "What does that mean?" "Well I think you're talking about, Matthew 15, around verses 22 or so. Well originally, everybody thought Christ came for the children of Israel, but soon learned He came for those that were not Jews too and they called them gentiles, which were those like you, Ami and myself," Mrs. Johnson explained. "Whatever they stood to inherit through the death, burial and resurrection of Christ, so did we, but with one stipulation," she said.

"What was that," Ami questioned? Both Rhonda and Mrs. Nosey looked quickly at her in shock. Rhonda had not realized before that moment Ami had taken just as much interest in *The Message* if not more, than she had. Seeing Ami's eyes light up let her know this was the missing piece she and Ami needed. Mrs. Johnson went on to explain, stuttering through her first word, "W... we...ll, first you had to hear the gospel, then you had to believe it, receive it by faith." Mrs. Johnson continued. "That is without seeing it actually happen and believe that it was God that came down in human flesh."

"He, being God, restraining the full measure of His power, to be a sacrifice for those that were lost because of what happened in the Garden of Eden, with Adam and Eve." She continued to explain as if she was telling a mysterious store. "He came, lived as a man and died for our sins, He was the sacrifice, like back when they use to kill animals once a year to ask God's forgiveness for anything, they or their family, did all year. Their sins, through those animals, where wiped out, never happened." She went on to say, "See, He was the ultimate sacrifice, because God in His infinite wisdom knew that taking a part of Himself and offering it up, for us would cover us forever. The blood of His Son, that which was taken from Himself, was pure, just like the lambs that knew no sin they use to sacrifice, Jesus knew no sin." Mrs. Johnson looked to make sure they were following and understanding the magnitude of what she was explaining.

She concluded, "Once He died on the cross, He was raised to life, by the power of God in Him. Because He did so well, in his journey and display of humility before us and God, His reward was to be Lord of all things in Heaven and in Earth, including you and me." She continued with emphasis. "If you believe that, the Gospel, and that He is Lord, once you confess it from your mouth, you inherit all salvation has to offer, including healing! Does that make sense?" Mrs. Johnson questioned as she turned nodding her head yes at them both.

Ami and Rhonda both sat quietly for a second taking in all that she had said, then Ami said with joy, "Well I believe Jesus is Lord, and He's so nice," as she picked up her fork and scooped a pile of peas. Rhonda and Mrs. Johnson both looked at her and wondered what she meant. Something in how she said it, made them feel she knew Him personally. As the evening progressed, Mrs. Johnson explained a little more about what it meant to walk with God; Grace, Mercy and Truth. Time flew by, and before they realized, it was time for bed.

Rhonda thought to herself that this was wonderful but knew she would have to call it a night. Mrs. Johnson said. "You know, you two should come and visit my church next Sunday." Rhonda, not realizing the words coming out of her mouth agreed, "We'd like that." She couldn't believe she said it. It happened so fast, but she liked the idea of knowing more about Christ, and if her church could give her more of what she was missing, she was all in. "Well, it's settled, I will see you two next Sunday morning about 10:15 a.m. I like to get there a little early for prayer," Mrs. Johnson said as she opened the door to leave. "That sounds fine, have a good night Ma'am," Rhonda said, as she closed the door behind Mrs. Johnson. She and Ami both new they would have a long day tomorrow, so they both decided it was time to ready for bed.

The next morning was rough for both Ami and Rhonda. They had to get back in the routine of normal life. This was hard after having so much time off from school and work. Even though Rhonda had Ami's classwork mailed to her so Ami would not fall behind, she knew Ami would have to face the scare of what happened to her at school that day. Even though Ami never said anything, she knew it was tough for her at school, because Ami only ever mentioned one real friend and that was Kianna.

As they started out the door for the school before-care program, Rhonda realized she had left her phone on silent all day the day before, so she and Ami could spend their last day on mini vacation without interruption. She giggled to herself as she located her phone and looked to see if their where any messages. She noticed an unknown number in her phone, which she was not concerned with, but she had also missed a call from Michelle. Deciding to wait and check her messages later, she placed the phone back in her purse after turning the ringer on and drove Ami to school..

Heading into work, she thought about all the things Mrs. Nosey had shared with her. It had been so long since anyone was a part of her life that was wise like her sister. She felt Mrs. Nosey was someone she could learn a lot from, but she had to get the name Mrs. Nosey out of her head if she was going to interact with her. She had already slipped up once and almost called her that instead of Mrs. Johnson.

She laughed out loud as she pulled into work, knowing she had missed all this time from work. There was no telling what mess she would find when she walked in. "Well, here we go," as she pulled the keys out of the car, grabbed her purse and bag and opened the car door.

The day went by rather quickly and before she knew it her shift was over. She headed home to cook dinner for Ami and realized she had not listened to her messages and she needed to call Michelle back. She was off that day for the first time after she covered her shift for two weeks. She located her phone as she sat in the car, "Hey girl, just calling to check on you two, hit me back when you get this." She knew Michelle was going to fuss her out when she returned her call, so she went in to listen to the next message. "Hello, this is Dr. Myles Johnson, I was just following up with Ami and her progress. Please give me a call at..oh shoot. Ummm.oh...657-984-7126. I look forward to speaking with you…"

Rhonda, in shock listened to the message again, and again until she almost had the number memorized. She thought to herself, "I'm not about to call this man, he can read Ami's chart. I can't believe that he is just calling to check on Ami. Frustrated that he had called, she slammed the phone back into her purse and started her car. Talking to herself and trying to find all the flaws she could about Dr. Johnson, she began to convince herself he was not worth her time, no matter how fine he was.

Settling in for the evening after dinner, she sat in the living room, thinking about her day. She decided to return Michelle's call and got her voice mail. She left a message and decided she would put some music on, she loved jazz, and this was a jazz kind of day. Turning the music on she heard her phone ringing on the coffee table, thinking to herself, "she would call when I'm trying to get my relax on". She picked up the phone and immediately recognized the number, it was the number Dr. Johnson had left for her.

Nervously she answered the phone, "Hello." A deep-toned voice responded, "Well hello Ms. Hodge, this is Dr. Myles. How are you and Ami this evening?" Rhonda, a bit shocked at how deep his voice was over the phone she answered nervously, "We are doing well, thank you for asking." "How is Ami adjusting to the medication I prescribed?" "She's doing ok on it; we haven't had any issues so far." "I know I told you I would call in a few days," Rhonda interrupted him midsentence, "No it's fine, I know doctors are busy." "No, that's not it, I just feel like I made you uncomfortable and I wanted you to settle on the idea of me calling you..." Dr. Myles said as he waited for her to respond.

There was a slight silence and he continued, "to check on Ami, of course, but also to see how you were holding up." Rhonda, not knowing what to say, there was such a calmness to his voice, and she remembered how fine he was, all the flaws she tried to convince herself he had went right out of her head. "Well, I appreciate that, but do you give all of your patients this much attention?" she questioned. "Well, no, but I do try to follow up with them after they visit the ER. You, however, are a special case. Let's just say I'm intrigued by your strength and want to make sure you're ok. What you went through was no small thing, but the way you handled yourself, piqued my interest in you as a person."

"Look," she said with a snap, "I don't know what you saw but I am not interested in allowing myself to be..., never mind. Thank you for calling to check on Ami, she is fine and so am I." "Ok, I won't keep you then. Please tell Ami hello for me and let her know I called to check on the two of you." "I will do that. Good night!" "Good night," he said clearing his throat as the line went dead.

Rhonda could not believe the nerve of this man. Angered by the conversation, she started to review what just happened. Feeling she had overreacted in the situation, she felt a heaviness in her chest, full of regret and fear. She didn't know what this feeling was, but she knew she had felt it only one time before, when she agreed to testify against John. Why was this doctor throwing her off her square so much? She had male pursuers before, but none of them made her this afraid.

She knew she had mishandled the situation with Dr. Myles, but she wasn't about to let it shake her anymore. She shook off the encounter and went in the room to check on Ami's progress of getting ready for bed. "Hey honey, you all ready for bed sweety?" "Yes Mommy. Who were you mad at on the phone,?" Ami asked with a strange look on her face. "No one baby. That was just Dr. Johnson, calling to check on you," she said as she sat down on the bed and grabbed Ami's covers to pull them over her. "Did he ask you out yet?" "What," Rhonda asked in surprise? "No, he did not and why are we having this conversation?" "Well, seems to me, you didn't let him, from what I heard!" Ami said in an 'I'm just saying' tone. "Ooow, little girl, sometimes you are too grown."

"Well Mommy, seems to me, we can't always run from love. Sometimes it's bound to find us." As Rhonda sat there in shock of the wise words coming out of the mouth of someone so young, she knew the words rang true. Was that what she was doing, or was she just protecting Ami and herself, by keeping things that they didn't need out? "Good night baby, I love you," she said, as she tucked the corners of the covers around her. Rhonda stood up, reaching to turn off the light, then she slowly left the room.

Rhonda walked down the hall to her bedroom thinking of what Ami had said to her. She also couldn't help but think of what Mrs. Johnson said to her the night before at dinner, "Well honey, this life you are living isn't going to live itself. You have to find time to work and play, can't be about business all the time!" She smiled as she entered the room. As she sat on the bed and Dr. Myles's voice replayed in her head, "Let's just say I'm intrigued by your strength and want to make sure you are ok." As her mind began to wander, she felt her smile become bigger - so much that she felt her cheeks getting a bit flushed, "The way you handled yourself piqued my interest in you as a person." "I have to hand it to him, he sure is smooth with it," she giggled a bit to herself, as she reached over and turned the light off. Nestled down in the bed, she began thinking "I sure hope this man don't show up in my dreams," and felt herself drifting off to sleep.

A BREATH OF FRESH AIR

It was a long night for Rhonda, though she was exhausted, she found herself laying there unable to stop her mind from racing most of the night. Dr. Myles was in her thoughts but soon she found herself drifting into her past, she would not allow herself to forget what she went through with James. As the night passed on, Rhonda finally drifted off to sleep and awoke the next morning feeling as though she had not slept at all. Still tired, she managed to get Ami to before care and made it to work on time. "Girl I know you got my message; I saw you called me back," Michelle said as she entered Rhonda's office.

Rhonda was the manager and often left her door open for her employees, which was something Sam did not approve of. "Yes, I left you a message, too. I figured it was too late for you to call me back, and then I got another call and …," Rhonda said, with a frustrated look, as she stood to pull something from the file cabinet in the corner of the room behind her. "Who calling you that late at night, do I need to be worried?" Michelle said with a grin. "Girl nobody, just Dr. Johnson, Ami's ER Doctor," Rhonda said sharply.

"Wait a minute, who is this doctor and why is he calling if he's the ER doctor, I didn't think they did stuff like …," as she paused for a moment, then continued, "Wait, he wasn't really calling about Ami. He wanted to chat with the fine, beautiful Ms. Hodge. I see, you betta' slay you a doctor, then girl!" Michelle said, as she moved in closer and sat down in the chair. Pulling it closer to the desk Rhonda had positioned herself behind, trying to act as though she was uninterested in the thought of talking about Dr. Myles.

"Spill it," Michelle demanded. Rhonda knowing Michelle could see right through her, "Girl it's nothing, he was just…," Rhonda trying to make light of the accusation by waving it off with her hand. "No Ma'am, something got you lookin' like you ain't slept all night, and I think it's this blow your mind kind of a man," Michelle said. "Girl he is fine," Rhonda said as if she was telling Michelle a secret. "Had to be, for you to be coming up in here looking the way you do this morning. Girl, at least fix your hair right." "So, what did he say," Michelle continued, "When y'all goin' out. I can watch Ami. All I'm saying is, it's about time, you been walkin' around here needing a little romance in ya life for far too long!" "We're not!" Rhonda replied abruptly.

"What! Well why the heck not, you said he was fine," Michelle a bit angered, "You didn't even let him ask you out did you?" she questioned. "To top it all off he's really a nice guy. I guess I'm just stuck in my past and I can't shake what I went through," Rhonda said, almost to the point of tears, realizing she may have missed an opportunity.

"The way I talked to him, girl he may never call again," Rhonda said. "Chile please, you not going to be able to keep a man like that away. If he can make it through medical school, that already says a lot about his will and determination," she laughed and continued, "you, honey, you are but a small feat," as they both giggled. Michelle walked over to hug Rhonda, "It will all work out, God has a way of putting things right when it seems everything is wrong." "Wait, what do you know about God?" Rhonda questioned. "I have been talking to my neighbor Ms. Nosey, I'm sorry, Mrs. Johnson, she gave me this message book and Ami and I have been reading it."

"First of all, Mrs. Nosey? Really," Michelle said with a laugh. "Why are you calling the lady Mrs. Nosey?" Michelle questioned as she continued laughing. "Girl, you only have to meet her one time to find out why. Better still pay more attention when you pull up to the building to know why, she is always watching and peeping," Rhonda said. "I'm sorry, I have to call her Mrs. Johnson now, she is a hot mess, but she is very wise too. She invited us to church with her Sunday," Rhonda explained, "in fact you want to come with?" "Girl no, my momma is all the Mrs. Nosey I need in this lifetime," Michelle said. "Sounds like you like this Mrs. Johnson, huh?" She concluded as she reached for a mint from the candy bowl on Rhonda's desk. "Yeah, took me a minute but she is growing on me," Rhonda said as she stood up.

"Girl it's just like you to get me in this office and get me started like we aren't at work, get your tail out of here and let me get back to it. This day will be gone before you know it!" They both laughed and Michelle turned to head out of the office. "Promise me, when Mr. Doctor man calls again you will give that man a chance and not be so darn mean all the time," she said with a look of concern in her eyes. "I mean it, now, just give him a chance Rhonda, you deserve to be happy."

Rhonda sat back down in her chair and thought about what Michelle said, in fact she thought of all the things which had been said to her over the last few weeks. Deciding to let all that go for the moment and focus on her work, she managed to make it through the day.

She and Ami finished the day off with a good read from *The Message*. She placed the book in the chair, deciding she had to get some much needed rest and turned in for the night.

THE PLACE OF HEALING

The days seemed to pass quickly and before she knew it, "Ami are you ready baby?" from inside the bathroom excitement rang out, "Yes!" Ami was in rare form, and Rhonda couldn't tell if it was just the excitement of trying something new or if Ami knew something she didn't. Strange things had been happening all morning as if the day had been already orchestrated for her. Somehow, she knew the exact outfit she was going to wear, earrings, shoes, and even down to the clutch purse. Not to mention, Ami came out of the bathroom looking as if she was an angel. Rhonda found herself feeling as if she was in a fairytale, but she didn't know who was telling the story.

Ready for what the day planned to offer, Ami and Rhonda headed downstairs and knocked on Mrs. Johnson's door. After several locks turned, Mrs. Johnson opened the door and stood in front of the two as if they all had coordinated their ensemble the day before. "Well, look at God," Mrs. Johnson said as she looked Rhonda over. "I love your dress suit Mrs. Johnson," Ami said with excitement! "Oh, my goodness, we all have on the same colors!" Ami said.

"Ami," Rhonda said quickly trying to quiet Ami. "It's ok, suga', she's just stating the obvious, let that child be free. Well I guess we are all ready, let's make it," Mrs. Johnson said as she grabbed her purse and keys.

Arriving at the church Rhonda felt a bit uncomfortable. Everyone was hugging on their way in and all around her there was chatter filled with laughter. Ami, ecstatic and wide eyed, watched Mrs. Johnson like a hawk and could not stop smiling. As they made their way down the right side of the room, Mrs. Johnson made her way to the seventh row and motioned for Rhonda to enter, "Ami, sweetie you can sit right by me, I want you close just in case you get the fidgets," she said.

As they all took their assigned seating a woman who seemed to be wearing the same colors as some of the other ladies, positioned at the doors of the church, walked over and handed Rhonda a pamphlet, "Well Good morning, Mrs. Intrusive," she said, with a sharp look on her face as she peered her eyes toward Mrs. Johnson. "Is this your niece, daughter or just a friend here?"

Rhonda's eyes widened and she tried not to laugh aloud, giggling to herself, forgetting not to let her body move. "You're the only one being nosey here, dear, and not that it is any of your business, but this is my neighbor, Ms. Hodge and her daughter Ami." "Is she one you trying to get to confess all they sin today," the woman said, as she turned to look at Rhonda. "No, dear I'm only trying to keep you from burning in Hell," Mrs. Johnson replied sharply. "Well honey I feel I better warn ya, you better hold on to your tea, Mrs. Johnson has a way of making you spill it." She said as she snatched her neck, turned and started to walk away.

Ami was still excited and looked at Rhonda laughing, "Mommy when are we getting the tea?" "Honey don't pay her no mind; I can't help it if she told me all her dirty little laundry!" "Huh," Mrs. Johnson said with a snark. "Then have the nerve to get mad with me, because I wouldn't introduce her to my son, Chile please," Mrs. Johnson continued, as she began to stand for the worship leader. "Ok, here we go," she said.

Ami really enjoying herself, turned to Mrs. Johnson and said. "Can we dance to it, I feel like dancing?" Mrs. Johnson laughing, looked at Ami, "You can do whatever you feel like doing suga, just be free." Rhonda quickly grabbing Ami's arm to stop her from break dancing in the aisles, whispered in Ami's ear quickly, "Just do it right here baby, let's leave a little in the tank for next time." "So, you thinking about coming back, huh," Mrs. Johnson said, as she faced forward. Rhonda thinking to herself, "How in the world did she hear me over the music and the singing, it's loud as heck in here!" "Yes, maybe." Mrs. Johnson continuing to clap her hands, "Well I always feel you have to give things more than one chance to decide if it is something you will enjoy anyway."

Worship started to slow down and so did Rhonda's heart, amidst all the noise she felt herself being pulled in by the lyrics of the songs being sung.

> In spite of my past mistakes, in spite of my guilt and shame, your love keeps calling out, out my name.

> No matter how much pain, your love keeps on chasing me, no matter how long it takes you reach for me.

> In your presence now, I can lay down my crown. You never turn a way; you just keep pursuing me.

> In you I find my home, I'm no longer alone. I made up my mind, no longer running from what's behind.

> You brought me to this place, your love covers my shame. And you know me by name.

> You called my name, you healed my pain, you make me whole, Jesus I'm yours.

> You called my name. From your secret place oh, God!

> You healed my pain, My past is no longer my shame!

> You make me whole, So Jesus, Jesus, I'm yours."

Rhonda's eyes filled with tears! She had not felt such passion and heaviness all at the same time. It was as if the words were her own and she could not hold back the tears any longer, she had to let them flow. Mrs. Johnson, recognizing the place Rhonda had come to in her heart, reached over and motioned for Ami, who also was full of tears, to move over. Something in her knew Rhonda needed her more than Ami at that moment. As Ami slid to the outside seat, Mrs. Johnson moved in and grabbed Rhonda by the hand, pulling her to her, as she embraced her for the remainder of the song.

When the song ended, the assistant pastor stood up and approached the podium, grabbed the microphone and began to praise as he taught through his tears. Mrs. Johnson released Rhonda, she had managed to keep her composure and stood to face the pastor. Rhonda gathering herself, grabbed the Kleenex Ami handed her from the box sitting in the seat in front of her. She carefully wiped her eyes (ensuring she preserved her makeup), face and then began to softly blow her nose.

"What a song, I don't think there is a dry eye in the building," he began to exclaim. "If that didn't grab your heart and turn it inside out, I don't know about you but I'm just," he paused. "I'm just undone!" He continued to exhort the congregation, "How many of you know God's love will chase you, and it doesn't matter what you have done or been through he still wants you? He calls you by name, He offers you salvation, and if that's not enough, He sanctifies you! Then the God that pursues you, he sends His Mercy, to every area of your life, where you still feel jacked up or the areas you struggle in. My God, and if that's not enough, He sends Grace in there to help you get where you need to be... Not one time but over and over again..." "What a mighty, loving God we serve..."

"He waits for us, He doesn't push His way in, He just keeps calling us by name, pursuing us in every situation, saying I'm here, I'm waiting, I'm willing to wait on you." Rhonda thought to herself, "I have to keep it together," fighting back the tears not knowing what was happening to her. But, she broke out into tears again. It was as if a floodgate had been opened and all she could do was sob on the shoulders of Mrs. Johnson. Mrs. Johnson held her from the waist. "That's alright Suga', you just let the Lord have it all baby, you been holding it all in for too long, just let it all go now."

Rhonda felt as though she was in the safest of places and began to sob even harder, and before she knew it the pastor was saying, "If God has covered your shame and touched your heart today, if you need a relationship with the Lord, I want you to come on down here I want to pray for you." Before Rhonda could step past Mrs. Johnson to go down, she noticed Ami's seat was empty. She and Mrs. Johnson stepped out into the aisle and looked down at the alter and Ami was already there.

Rhonda could not believe her eyes, she started to cry seeing that even Ami was touched by the service, although she didn't understand how someone so young could possibly understand what was going on in there. She knew Ami was not the average child. As she made her way to the alter, she felt a weight lifting from her, even from her heart, and even though she didn't know why, she felt like something was lifting off her. She knew it felt right and it felt good.

As the pastor began to pray Rhonda and Ami grabbed hands, Rhonda reached over to grab Mrs. Johnson's hand and pull her close, "Say these words with me," he said. "Lord Jesus, I know You want me, I can see now that You have been with me, waiting on me. I give You all my past, all my pain, all my shame, all my hurt, all my disappointments," he continued. "Come into my heart, be my Lord and Savior, I give you my life, make me whole. In Jesus Name, Amen! Amen, Amen," he said as the worship team began to sing, everyone weeping at the altar, Rhonda, Ami and Mrs. Johnson returned to their sets. He began to preach the sermon, after the singing and gave one final alter call.

"Is it over," Ami questioned, "I could stay here all day," she said as they gathered their belongings. "Yes, Dear, the service is over, but your walk with the Lord has just started!" Mrs. Johnson assured. "Well, good, I like my walk with Him so far!" Ami said with a huge smile on her face. "What's next," Ami said with excitement." "Home, young lady, home. Mrs. Johnson, I think we have created a fanatic!" Rhonda said as she grabbed Ami by the hand as everyone began to leave. "I sure hope so," Mrs. Johnson was smiling and laughing with Rhonda as they headed out of the sanctuary.

The ride home was quiet, and they all seemed to need some rest, by the time they entered the apartment building Ami was already yawning. "Well I hope you both enjoyed yourselves, I know I did," Mrs. Johnson said as she headed to her door. "We truly did, thank you for having us," Rhonda said as she headed towards the stairs which led to her apartment. "You just let me know if you want to go again next Sunday, I don't want to be pushy or anything, I'll just let you decide," Mrs. Johnson said.

Before Mrs. Johnson could finish her sentence, Ami interjected, "Oh yes, we would love to, Right mommy?" "Well I guess Ami has spoken!" Rhonda said as she laughed. "Yes, we wouldn't miss it, thank you so much for today," she said with a humble tone in her voice. "Honey just thank God that He knows your name," Mrs. Johnson said as she turned to place the key in the door. "Alright, you both have a good evening and I'll be seeing you," she concluded, as she unlocked the two outer locks on her door, to opened it while Rhonda and Ami began to walk the stairs.

The weeks went by and faithfully every Sunday, Rhonda and Ami would make their way to church and sit in their usual assigned seats. Rhonda was now feeling a bit more confident in what she believed, began to make her way down to the alter occasionally for prayer. Ami would follow at times until one day Rhonda felt confident enough to say a prayer to God for herself. The two of them had spent many evenings in study of the message with Mrs. Johnson and what she did not obtain an understanding of at church, she would always inquire with Mrs. Johnson, after being advised to take detailed notes. Before long, Rhonda's faith was flourishing and she felt she had taken a turn towards a new life and a newfound Joy, in her relationship with God.

BREAKTHROUGH

As service ended one Sunday morning, after just a few months of attending church on a regular basis, Ami leaned over as service was ending and asked Rhonda with a whisper, "Mommy, may I go and say hi to Doctor Johnson?" Rhonda a bit puzzled, quickly looked at Ami and said, "What? Where, is he here?" "Yes Mommy, he's here most Sundays, but he never stays or comes to the front," she whispered. "He leaves before everybody else," Ami said none silently.

"Well, where is he honey?," Rhonda asked as she tried to find him in the crowd of now standing people, "I don't see him. I don't see him now, I guess he left," Ami said, as Rhonda grabbed her chest as if to slow down the beating of her heart. Rhonda wondered if it was him and why he had not come to say hello, but then, why would he, the way she talked to him on the phone. "Who ya'll lookin for," Mrs. Johnson asked as she tried to follow Rhonda's eyes. "Oh, no one just someone we met a while back, Ami thought she saw," Rhonda explained. "Well it was him, he just left though," Ami said with disappointment. "It's ok baby, we will catch him another time," Rhonda assured.

"Oh, I see, it's a 'him' we are looking for," Mrs. Johnson said with a giggle in her voice. "Mrs. Johnson, leave it alone. We are just finishing up service and here you go, can we just let the Lord rest on us today," Rhonda said as they both begin to laugh. "Well, I guess you're right, we should just let Him rest." She said then changing the conversation quickly asked, "How about you and Ami come for dinner next Saturday? Well, I have to make sure I'm still off work, but that sounds nice, be nice to eat someone else's cooking for a change," Rhonda replied, "Besides you owe us for barging in on us a few months back." "Well, I guess you are right, honey, but how else was I going to get you here?"

As they all began to laugh and hug each other they began to exit the church. "Well, we will see you later. Ami and I are going to visit with some friends," Rhonda told her, as they turned to walk towards Rhonda's car. "Ok, have a wonderful afternoon, see ya'll later," Mrs. Johnson said loudly, as the distance began to grow between them. Walking to the car Rhonda could not help but look around the parking lot, hoping to catch a glimpse of the man Ami thought she had seen in the church; wondering was it really Dr. Myles.

The ride to Michelle's house seemed longer than usual. Rhonda couldn't wait to get to Michelle. She needed to do some serious venting and to tell her that Ami thought she saw Dr. Myles at church. Michelle and Raymond didn't have any children, but Michelle made sure her nieces, Stacy and Gail, were there for Ami to play with. She didn't want

Ami to feel bored or uncomfortable especially when she knew that Rhonda and she could sit and talk for hours and never look up. Michelle was good that way, she was always thinking about what was best for other people and very wise beyond her years. Michelle was about 5 foot seven, long natural hair with dreadlocks, amber colored skin, and voluptuously full lips. She didn't hold any punches when it came to her opinion and that is what Rhonda loved about her. She knew she wouldn't spill the tea if she told her anything, it was a bond most would say was from heaven.

Michelle and she would often get together and talk for hours without interruption, except the few times Raymond would answer a random doorbell. Raymond hated the fact that Rhonda was as beautiful as she was and didn't have someone looking after Ami and her. He loved the way that Rhonda loved his wife and wanted her to be happy. He often tried to fix her up with some of his guy friends. She would ignore his attempts as he would often have one of his friends just happen to stop by unannounced. Over time, it became very obvious what he was trying to do. Explaining to Michelle, he thought Rhonda may be interested each time. This had gone on for us a couple of years. After a while, Michelle told him to stop, God would work out Rhonda's love life and he was no matchmaker.

When Rhonda finally pulled up to the house Michelle came to the door to meet her and Ami. She was so excited to see them, "bout time! Get in here, Ami. The girls are in the backyard," she yelled. As they both approached the door she began to laugh, "What's so funny," Rhonda questioned. "I was just wondering, did y'all have a nice service with Mrs. No, I mean, Johnson?" she asked as she opened the door hugging Ami and let her pass. "Hello baby" as she grabbed her quickly and passed her on by. "Hello," Ami managed to yell out as she darted towards the backyard.

Rhonda still giggling to herself looked at Michelle shaking her head, "You gon' quit that," they both laughed, Rhonda shook her head, "Yes, it was very nice, but we'll talk about that in a minute." Rhonda said with a 'we need to talk' expression on her face. "That doesn't sound good. You want your usual glass of wine first or you want something else to drink? Ami, you want a snack or something to drink?," Michelle yelled, "Cause it sound like your mom is not going to need any interruptions in a few minutes," she said under her breath. "No ma'am, I'm ok right now," Ami yelled from outside. "Ok baby, it's really good to see you Ami," she said as she made her way into the kitchen.

Michelle turned the corner and approached the kitchen area, "Come on in here girl, I'm in the kitchen fixing dinner." "Where is Raymond?" Rhonda asked. "Oh girl, in the man cave," Michelle said giving a look of yeah right. "I sure hope, girl, please tell me he didn't invite some random stranger here to meet me. This is not the day for that", Rhonda said as she gave a sigh. "Oh, you do need that glass of wine," Michelle said as she moved to the wine glasses in the cabinet, "Girl I told Raymond to stop doing that mess, the last time he did it," as they both laughed and headed toward the dining room.

Rhonda couldn't wait to spill, blurting out, "Hurry up and sit-down girl, I have something to tell you!" "What girl," they were both acting like two school aged girls still in high school with secrets they could only share with each other. "Well we're sitting in church and Ami leans over and whispers to me, "Dr. Myles is at the church! I'm looking all around for this man all obvious like..." "You don't think he's been coming to the church," Michelle interrupted. "Well, apparently, she's seen him there several times and she said he always leaves before service is over. I'm wondering, if this man has been there this whole time and has not said anything to me!" "Well Rhonda you didn't really give the man a half of a chance the last time, can you blame him?" Michelle said sarcastically. "It could be he is just letting you worship in peace or maybe he's waiting for the right moment, you never know."

"Well let me ask you this, what are you gonna do if he does come up and talks to you?" "I really don't know, probably pass out," Rhonda said. "Well, if it is him, I think you should just stay calm and let it play out, but it sounds to me, like you want to give Dr. Myles a chance?" "I don't know, maybe I do?" Rhonda said as though she was still unsure, but Michelle knew there was something much deeper to Rhonda's resistance when it came to men. Although this was the first time, she had ever seen Rhonda this shaken by someone. "What, help me understand, you the one who obviously has a thing for this man." "I mean just from your description of him alone, he is someone you're interested in," she said frustratedly.

"What's holding you back?" Michelle still sounding frustrated with Rhonda continued. "I mean every guy that has ever asked you out, in the past three years that I have known you, you've turned them down," she said with elevated voice. "Now something else is going on, you are too beautiful and too young to be this closed off." Michelle, seeing tears well up in Rhonda's eyes, began to calm herself, changing her tone. "I know you told me that things didn't go so well in your last relationship with Ami's father, but you can't let whatever happened, stop you from ever being happy," Michelle paused to get a response from Rhonda. "Michelle if I told you what happened, I think you would better understand..." Rhonda paused for a moment as if to hold herself together, "why I try so hard to push people away, separating myself from anything I think would remotely make me happy."

Michelle looked at Rhonda's face, seeing the pain in her eyes. She could tell Rhonda had a lot more to talk about than just some guy who broke her heart. They went into the living room after Michelle checked her dinner, looked to see where Raymond was, insuring there would be no interruptions. She walked to the patio door and if the girls were okay, then turned to Rhonda and they both sat down in the living room. As Rhonda sat down, she started to tell Michelle of her past. How she came to be in a witness protection program, how Ami's father was in the beginning, and how he had changed over time. She explained how his life of crime over time managed to change him and he became someone she didn't even recognize. She told her of how he was in college and the complete change in him after he went into business with his partner after college.

Michelle could hardly believe her ears, struggling to grasp every detail. As Michelle sat there with her mouth wide open, Rhonda was trying not to cry as she was rehashing things she had only replayed in her mind a million times but never been able to share with anyone. Michelle felt as though she understood why Rhonda was so careful, when it came to include her or anyone else in her life. She was grateful Rhonda was sharing and now she felt she had all the missing pieces to the puzzle. Although she could not relate to Rhonda's fears, she could now understand the need she had to keep Ami and herself safe.

After a while of crying, she and Michelle decided it was time for dinner. Michelle went to call the girls in, then went to get Raymond, who had left them alone all this time. He was engulfed in a football game, and food would be the only thing to pull him out of his "safe space" of his man cave. Once everyone was settled at the table, dinner was served. They spent the evening laughing, teasing and chatting about everyday life, Michelle often giving Rhonda the 'are you ok?' look. Rhonda, now feeling unburdened, was in a wonderful mood, not to mention she had two glasses of wine instead of her usual one. Needless to say, she needed them both.

Ami and Rhonda were exhausted by the end of the evening and decided it was time to head home. When they finally made it home Rhonda went to bed thinking about Dr. Myles. She thought about him possibly being at church this morning and why he didn't speak (if he had been there all those other Sunday's). She felt she had missed her opportunity with him, wondering if she would ever get the opportunity to find out if she was ready for something remotely resembling happiness with anyone, much less someone she had treated so harshly. She didn't know how to allow someone into Ami and her life, and if she would have the opportunity to find out one day. She finally drifted off to sleep, resolving in her mind that Dr. Myles had not known they were there and maybe it was something she should not continue to ponder.

PUTTING IT ALL TOGETHER

The week went by quickly, Saturday was fast approaching, Rhonda had almost forgotten about dinner with Mrs. Johnson. Rhonda had already started to plan out Saturday's chores on Friday night, and woke up Saturday to greet Ami with a kiss telling her of the busy morning she had planned for the two of them. Until Ami made mention of the evening, "Mommy I wonder what Mrs. Johnson's food is going to taste like tonight." Rhonda realized, she had completely forgotten the invitation, "Oh my gosh, I almost forgot we are supposed to have dinner with her!"

Thinking to herself if she had anything to take as a present for the invitation she now regretted accepting, "Thank you Ami, Lord knows we don't need that lady on our tops for forgetting," she said, as she checked to see if she had a spare bottle of wine to go with dinner. "Ahhh… no mom, leave the hip talk for us youngsters, just say 'on our heads'," Ami said sassingly, they both laughed and continued to fix breakfast.

When breakfast was over Ami retreated to her room for some light reading and play time with her dolls, doing all the things she loved to do on Saturday morning. Her birthday was just a few Sunday's away and though she wasn't expecting any gifts, due to her long stay in the hospital, she was still excited to go to Michelle's house to hang out with the girls and have cake.

Later that evening Ami and Rhonda managed to get themselves together, Rhonda had on a light sun dress with sandals, and just a touch of makeup for a natural look of beauty, finished off with a little lip gloss. As they made their way downstairs to Mrs. Johnson's apartment, Rhonda started to get excited to spend time with her newfound friend, she was turning into somewhat of a mother figure to her and she was just as smart mouthed if not more than her mother. Rhonda made sure Ami's hair and dress was pleasing to the eye as they approached the hallway, knocking on the door.

They both started to get excited, because the smell coming out into the hallway made them even hungrier than they were before. As they stood there hearing the first lock, they waited patiently, after 5 locks there stood Mrs. Johnson. Opening the door, she invited Rhonda and Ami in with a smile, "I hope you guys don't mind, but my son stopped by and I asked him to stay for dinner." Rhonda's face changed quickly, feeling this was a setup, "What?" "No... we can come back another time." She said as Mrs. Johnson walked towards the dining area.

She had a strange happy mood about her that they had not seen before, which made them feel welcome. There was an overwhelming feeling they both had immediately started to overtake them both, like the first time they went to Michelle's house for a barbeque. Rhonda knew there was something special about this lady and she loved spending time with her, so she let it go for the moment. This was something Rhonda didn't feel very often, and she wasn't willing to let the circumstances stop her from eating some of this good smelling food and spending time with someone she was beginning to hold very dear.

As they walked the hallway, she started to feel somewhat at home. It had been sometime since they had felt this way with a stranger. Rhonda was now feeling like she was with her family again for a moment but didn't like being set up. Mrs. Johnson, happy they were there, was hoping Rhonda would stay and said, "Oh, heavens no, I made plenty, more than enough in fact maybe too much." Now, he's in the bathroom but he won't bother you, he's a real sweetheart, trust me. Besides, he probably can't stay long anyway, he's always getting calls telling him something is going wrong and he needs to leave at a moment's notice. You two come this way, he will be out shortly, but dinner is ready," she assured as she ushered them in to the neatly arranged dining room.

Hearing the bathroom door opening, Rhonda began to get nervous, she could hear the door open and someone coming down the hallway. Suddenly she could hear a man's voice which sounded somewhat familiar, but she could not place it. "Mom, who is it at the door," he asked from down the hallway? "We're in the dining room, son, that was just my neighbor," she said with elevated voice. "She and her daughter are here for dinner, remember I told you somebody else was coming for dinner," "Well I didn't believe you'" he said with a laugh, still a way off from the dining room door.

Rhonda, still trying to place the man's voice, had dropped her napkin on the floor and reached down to pick it up as a man came around the corner wiping his hands with a paper towel, holding his head down checking his pants while looking down and the top of his head and body frame was all you could see. Rhonda thinking to herself, man he sounds fine, reaching for the table to pull herself upright. She could tell she knew that voice but couldn't place it, until he walked into the dining room and lifted his head. Rhonda looked up and almost fell out of her chair!

"Mommy," Ami begin to smile very big, it was Dr. Myles! Rhonda had never put the two together because she always called him Dr. Myles and didn't figure Mrs. Johnson had a doctor for a son. First, there are so many Johnson's in the world why would she think they were related, much less mother and son. Rhonda, stood to her feet while Mrs. Johnson was wondering what was going on here, started introducing him, "Rhonda, Ami, this is my son Myles."

Rhonda still speechless, stood there with her mouth open. Ami, over excited to see Dr. Myles jumped from the table, ran over and gave him a hug. Mrs. Johnson shocked by this, "Well I'll be doggone, y'all know each other!" Rhonda still quite speechless, managed to mutter the words, "Yes, we do. Hello Dr. Johnson," she stuttered. His eyes fixed on her even while Ami was hugging his legs, just as surprised as they were, said with a deep voice, "Good evening Ms. Hodge."

"Well I be doggone, I didn't know y'all knew each other or this would've happened a long time ago. Come on now, let's eat," Mrs. Johnson said, now even more excited about the evening. Everyone took a seat at the table, "I don't want to make anyone uncomfortable mom, Myles said, still gazing at Rhonda, "I can go if it does?" Rhonda spoke before Mrs. Johnson could say anything, "No one is uncomfortable, please stay." Dr. Myles shocked by her quickness, started smiling from ear to ear, "Ok," he said, with a puzzled look on his face. "Well, there you have it, she wants you to stay," Mrs. Johnson said, with a meddling tone.

Dinner that evening wasn't full of a lot of chatter, in fact there wasn't much talking at all. Aside from Mrs. Johnson and Ami talking back-and-forth, laughing and cutting eyes at Rhonda and Dr. Myles, who couldn't seem to take their eyes from each other. Ami and Rhonda sat watching the two of them as if they were bird watching, giggling to themselves, as they are cutting glances throughout the entire meal. This was entertainment enough when Mrs. Johnson finally broke the silence, "Well, I'm finding it awful funny. God sure works in mysterious ways." Rhonda said, with a smile, admittingly, "Well I guess he does." Everyone was smiling and deciding that dinner was over, rose from the table and retreated to the living room.

Making themselves comfortable, Myles made sure that he sat across the room with Ami so he could continue to stare at Rhonda. Mrs. Johnson served coffee and tea for Ami. Ami, going overboard with the sugar, quickly got a, "that's enough," from Rhonda. "Now how you going to tell her how she likes her tea," Mrs. Johnson asked.

"Mom, that is her child, now you cut that out, Myles said politely. "Ok, son, I will behave," she smiled and turned to Ami, "Do you want to see all the old fashion dolls I collected over the years, come back here in my den, if that is alright," she questioned. "Sure," Rhonda replied, she knew how much Ami loved dolls, "I can come too?" Mrs. Johnson, shooing her off, "I didn't invite you. See Ami, back here in the den is where I store them. Come on and I'll show you." Mrs. Johnson knew exactly what she was doing, managed to get Ami away from Rhonda and Dr. Myles, so they could talk.

"How have you been, Myles asked as he cleared his throat, "I mean, you and Ami, that is, I assume she's getting better." "We've been doing pretty good, yes she is getting better, it's been a journey," Rhonda said. They both were still quite nervous, pushing their way through, knowing for sure that now, they were being set up. "I hope you really didn't mind me staying for dinner, I know the last time we talked, you didn't want to have anything to do with me."

Rhonda started to feel a bit embarrassed as he reminded

her of her behavior on the phone, "I'm so sorry about that, I was just in a bad headspace and needed to let go of some things." Myles was feeling her sensuality, "I understand that, I figured there was something going on, I mean you didn't seem like the type of woman that would shoot my plane down out of the sky," he said with a slight chuckle. "I don't know, at least not without a parachute," Rhonda said, as they both laughed.

"So where are you from Ms. Hodge?" Myles questioned. The best answer Rhonda could think to give with hesitancy, "the south." "Oh yeah, where in the south?" Myles was seemingly over interested. "Rhonda quickly responded and changed the subject, "Oh you wouldn't know it, it's so small." "So, what made you become a doctor," she questioned. "Well I love people and I love medicine, so I really had no choice." Rhonda, overly interested as to distract Myles from asking her any questions about her past managed to keep the conversation as superficial as she possibly could, but she knew she would have to decide one day on whether to share her past with him, or not. This was not the type of man to deserve anything less than the truth, the whole truth and nothing but the truth and she knew it. Something in both of their eyes seem to light up and Rhonda couldn't help feeling swept away by his deep voice and smooth body language. This man was trouble in the worst way, and she knew it.

After some time with Myles and Rhonda's many attempts to catch her breath during their conversation, Ami and

Mrs. Johnson emerged from the back of the apartment giggling to themselves. "Well Ami, I have truly enjoyed you sweetie," said Mrs. Johnson, "but I'm an old lady and I need my rest." "Ahhh, I'm having so much fun, I'm not ready to go home. Are you mommy?" she and Mrs. Johnson secretly passed a wink and smile at each other trying not to giggle out loud. "Mommy can we walk the neighborhood or something, I would say go for ice cream but I'm still full of the pecan pie."

Myles interrupted before Rhonda could respond, "That would be nice. I would love to walk with you two." "I'm sure you would," Mrs. Johnson cut in, "Son, lock my door on your way out. You got the key." "Yes ma'am," as he rose to kiss his mother on the cheek. "Ok, Good night Rhonda..." she said really slow and grinning from ear to ear. "Good night Mrs. Johnson, and thank you for having us, it was wonderful." "I know it was - especially that surprise 6'4" dessert that showed up," she mumbled under her breath with a grin as she winked at Ami and walked down the hall.

Rhonda and Myles were both feeling a bit embarrassed but also knowing there was truth in the words she spoke, turned to look at each other and with a smile. Myles said, "Yeah, let's take that walk." As Ami and Rhonda gathered their things Rhonda realized she had to-go plates to take upstairs that Mrs. Johnson so graciously forced her to take. "I just have to run upstairs and place these plates in the fridge, you don't mind waiting, do you?" "Of course, not,"

Myles said with a smile. Ami however was rolling her eyes almost to the back of her head.

"This will take a while," she said, "her *moment* is to check her hair, lips and other unmentionable parts." "Ami! If you don't button that lip," Rhonda interrupted her mid-sentence, "Please excuse her, she does have manners." "It's quite alright," he said with a chuckle, "we'll wait here," as he continued to laugh and look at Ami, then turned to watch Rhonda walk up the stairs. He couldn't help but smile as he watched her take every step with ease as if the air was causing her to float up each step.

When Rhonda returned, Myles moved towards the door and held it open for the both of them, "Well that didn't take long at all, everything must have still been well put together, at least from what I could see it was." They both laughed as Myles looked her up and down like a lion spying his prey. Rhonda now was a bit self-conscious and started to rub her dress down and pat her hair to make sure she really was put together, "You know I was just joking right," Myles assured as they both giggled.

"You know, I'm going to have to watch you," Rhonda says with a big smile. "So, I take it I'm going to get the opportunity for you to do that, huh?" Myles asked excitedly as he sped up to get a couple of steps in front of her. He turned to see the look on her face when she answered his question. "Well, I'm thinking about it," Rhonda said as she realized Ami was almost a block ahead of them walking, "Ami, honey slow down and wait for us." "I did, I can't help if ya'll old and walk slow mommy," she yelled back. "That girl," Rhonda said as she shook her head and they both began to laugh again.

The walk seemed to come to an end so quickly, everything seemed so new and so fresh in the neighborhood to Rhonda, maybe it was because she and Ami didn't take many walks outside. Most of their outdoor adventures were with Michelle and her family at the park or an outdoor work event. This was a new experience and Rhonda was almost sad when the evening started to appear, she knew this was coming to an end and Myles had yet to inquire if she would see him again. As they made their way back to the apartment complex Rhonda started to get nervous, she didn't know how the evening would play out and the end was soon approaching.

She called to Ami and told her, "Go ahead and take this key, I'll be up in a moment", as they approached the door of the building. Myles seemed a bit nervous to her as well, "Are y'all 'bout to kiss, because I don't want to see that," Ami said as Rhonda gasped for air and choked on the soft drink they had stopped to get at the local store before they headed home. "Girl, I can't believe you, today! Get your tail in there. I'm so sorry," she said completely embarrassed.

"Don't be," Myles said as he smiled uncontrollably, "She's a child. Besides, I was wondering the same thing," as he let his laugh come forth. "Again, I'm just kidding, but I would like to do this again. This was very nice," he said as he paused for a moment, then continues, "As a matter of fact," Rhonda's eyes now wide and her body language a bit guarded, she knew there was no way she was going to kiss this man, no matter how full his lips or how gorgeous that smile was, "How about I take you out this Friday if you're free? Only if you want to, though, I don't want to push," he said as he raised his hands making a pushing motion towards her. "I think I would like that," she said with ease. There was something about this man. Everything seemed so easy, she had responded before she knew she had. Feeling a bit shocked by her own response, she quickly added, "But let me check my work schedule and get back to you." "You do that," he said. "I'm going to let you go and check on your princess and I will talk to you soon.?" "Yes, I will call you," Rhonda replied as she opened the door and walked through it. "Ok Goodnight!" Myles said as he turned and jogged down the stairs heading for his car.

SPILL IT

Entering the apartment, Rhonda realized she had left her phone on the table since she had been in such a hurry to return to Myles and Ami for their walk. She closed the door and heard a chime that she was receiving a text message. It was from Mrs. Johnson, "I hope you both enjoyed your dinner, I truly enjoyed myself. I hope the walk was delightful, it's about time you let yourself walk in the sun." She smiled as she remembered how beautiful the afternoon air was and how long it had been since she had enjoyed the sun that much but maybe it was more about the company than it was about the weather.

As she continued to check her phone, she saw she had two missed calls from Michelle. Rather than listening to her messages she hit the call back button on her phone, she could not wait to tell her what happened. "Hello," Michelle answered on the other end of the line. "Girl!" "You are not going to believe what I am about to tell you!" Rhonda said. Michelle could feel the excitement through the phone, "What girl, spill it!"

Rhonda began to tell Michelle of all the events which had

taken place and she could not believe her ears. "So, did he ask you out again!" Michelle asked, even more excited than Rhonda. Raymond walked by and asked, "Who you on the phone with?" Rhonda froze on the phone and could not speak. All the memories flooded her heart of the last words John said to her. It was as if she could feel his presence somehow, fear swept over her like the beginning of a storm.

Something in how Raymond said those words flooded her with emotions she had not felt in a long time. "Rhonda, Rhonda, you there, did he ask you out, girl. What's wrong? Michelle asked, "You got awful quiet. Now listen you been waiting for this man a long time, don't clam up now." Rhonda, coming to herself, hesitated for a moment, "Yes, I'm here and he did ask me out, but I didn't want to be too eager so I told him I would have to check my work schedule and get back with him later in the week." "Okay, that's good, so when you going to call him, or is he supposed to call you?" "I'm going to call him," Rhonda replied. "Okay, so what's going on with you right now, something in your voice changed," Michelle asked.

Rhonda, a bit nervous now, "Girl I don't know, but I just had this feeling like something is about to happen, you know that eerie feeling like something isn't right in that moment?" "Girl, everything is going to be fine, all of this is working itself out, and that man is in hot pursuit of you." Michelle assured her, "Just take it slow. Besides, he is a patient man, heck he's going to have to be dealing with you." Michelle said as they both laughed. "No, that's not it, but well, maybe you're right, maybe I'm just nervous about how all of this happened and the fact that he is of all people, Mrs. Johnson's son."

"I just can't believe I didn't pick up on it. She never said a word about who her son was or that he attended the same church as her," Rhonda went on to say. "Did you ask him if that was him," Michelle questioned. "No, girl I was so caught up in that smile and that voice, my head was spinning, I couldn't think to do anything but keep my legs moving so I didn't faint. Girl, the Lord was with me, I managed to keep it together," Rhonda said jokingly.

"Wow!" Michelle said. "Wow, what, Michelle?" "Girl that's the first time I have ever heard you talk about the Lord like that," Michelle said. "I know, right, I don't know, Michelle. It's like He is showing me the places in my life where He has been keeping me safe and loving me. These last months of church and hanging out with Mrs. Johnson, I guess you can say it's changing me. It's as if I know everything will be ok, and I feel stronger and better equipped to handle life, I'm just not as afraid anymore," Rhonda said with eyes full of tears.

"Man, listening to you talk right now is like I'm talking to a new person with a new lease on life," said Michelle. "This is definitely different, I'm so used to encouraging you and trying to push you to enjoy your life, I'm almost, and I do mean almost, because you know I have words for days, but I'm almost speechless!" As they both laughed and continued to talk about Rhonda's evening, Michelle realized it was getting late and they both had to be up for work in the morning.

"Well girl, I am so happy your man found you and, shoot, he came to get his woman," Michelle laughed as she continued to say, "In all seriousness, Rhonda, don't be afraid of how God wants to bless you, you are a beautiful woman inside and out, God loves you and so do I." As they both laughed Rhonda agreed and said, "Let's talk tomorrow girl, I need to go wash any bugs off I may have gotten from that long walk, and I need a hot bath. Girl, I hadn't realized how out of shape I am, my muscles are on ten right now, they hurt."

"I bet you do, but you might want to make it a cold shower," they both laughed, "No I'm serious, they say cold is better for those deep muscles you can't see, to settle them down." "Michelle!" Rhonda says. "You are a hot mess!" they both continued to laugh, "Alright girl, I will talk to your fast tail later," Michelle says. "Me fast, you with your potty mouth," Rhonda said laughingly, "OK, good night!" "Good night, cold shower, cold as you can stand it!" Michelle continued to laugh. "Bye, Michelle!"

As Rhonda prepared for bed, she reminisced over how the day was with Myles and Ami. She could picture herself having a happy life, with all the things which had happened over the last few months. It was somewhat scary to think of, given all the things she had gone through in her past. Keeping Ami safe was the most important thing to her, but

Myles was so caring it was hard not to wonder what life would be like now that he had entered the picture. After thinking on things a few minutes, her mind started to wonder back to the feeling she had when she was on the phone with Michelle.

It was a feeling she knew too well, and it frightened her something terrible. It was as if she knew something was about to happen and she couldn't shake it. She thought about what the pastor had said on Sunday, "God never leaves His people in the dark, He will always put a knowing in your spirit, and when He does, your job is to pray and ask for protection and for the will of God to be done in your life."

She remembered these words so clearly because as he spoke them it was as if he was speaking to her directly, "Remember, God makes all things new, old things are passed away, but with the process of life in every situation you find yourself in there is a lesson, and some of those lessons require forgiveness and letting go of past offenses and hurts, you cannot take the old things into what God is trying to make new in your life." Those words brought tears to her eyes even as she thought on them now. How was she to let go and forgive? She didn't know, but from what she was seeing about God at this point, she knew in her heart He would help her and she would find out.

"Ami honey, it's time to get up," Rhonda's voice echoed from the hallway as she entered Ami's room. She saw the book she had been reading to Ami on her pillow. As she grabbed the book and closed it, she placed it on the chair with the neatly folded blanket. "Ami?" she said as she rubbed her head, grabbing her long curls and pulling them over her back. "Yes, Mommy I'm awake." "Hey, baby", she said as she smiled and continued to rub Ami's head and hair, "I see you have been reading *The Message?*" "Yes, I read it every day," Ami answered still groggy with sleep. "Oh, wow, baby, I'm so proud of you," Rhonda said with amazement. "Yeah, Mommy, He said I would know Him if I remain in His word, He is His word," Ami replied with a flippant response.

Rhonda sat there with shock on her face, she didn't know if Ami had read this in the message or if she had personally spoken with God. She had read in the message, how Jesus gave gifts to men, some teachers, some preachers, some apostles, prophets and evangelists. Also, how people, could speak face to face with God on a personal level, but this was different. In fact, a lot of the things Ami had been saying over the last few months made her feel as though she was obtaining information on a personal level from God, Himself. Although it pleased her to hear Ami speak this way, she wasn't sure what it all meant.

Brushing the conversation off, she informed Ami she needed to hurry, because she wanted to get to work early this morning. She was excited about the day, as they prepared to leave. It wasn't because she expected anything great from the work she would be doing, but she knew she would be finding time to make that one phone call, yes, the call to Dr. Myles. She was eager to tell him she would love to go out with him Friday night or any other night after that. She knew she had it bad for this tall chocolate sip of mocha coffee and would find it hard to keep her composure. But she was determined not let on, she was feeling him and would try her best not to let it show.

HIDDEN MYSTERY IN PLAIN SIGHT

When she got to work, the first thing she did was check her schedule to make sure she was free Friday night. She thought about what she would do with Ami for the evening. This was a first for Rhonda and she didn't know how Ami would feel if she went out on a date with Myles. It had been just she and Ami for so long she wasn't sure how to do this, she knew Ami liked him though, and that made all the difference.

For most of the day she continued to work trying to pick the perfect time to call Myles and aside from the few distractions which came with the job, and the eight times Michelle would pass by her office, "You called him yet?" her day was pretty smooth. She noticed people staring at her for some reason, she couldn't figure out why, so she would leave the floor and retreat to her office. As she passed one of her employee's she spoke to her and asked her how she was doing. She was not ready for the response she gave and began to blush for the first time in a long time.

"I'm fine, how are you Ms. Happy?" Rhonda could not believe her ears, "What?" she said as she laughed with a big smile. "You are fluttering around here singing and smiling, I don't think anyone here has ever seen you like this. What's got your day so bright? Everybody has noticed and are talking about it." The young lady said with a sassy smile. "Well, I think I'm just learning to walk in the sun," Rhonda said. She was floored by the response and had not realized she had been singing all day. "Well it must have some extra vitamin D in it cause I ain't never seen the sun do you like that! Where he at? Maybe we all need to go stand in his sunshine for a minute," she said as Rhonda walked away.

As she made her way back to her office, she passed Sam in the hall, "Hey Sam." "Hey, he replied with his more than usual grump. "What's wrong with you," Rhonda asked. "Too happy around here. Maybe you should do some work, coming in here smiling and singing," he mumbled under his breath as she continued down the hallway to her office. She walked over to her desk and sat down, when she looked up Michelle was coming through the door and closed it.

"Girl, Sam is hot with you honey," Michelle said as she took her usual seat. "Why, I been working all day, I don't know what his problem is," Rhonda said with attitude, "I ain't thinking about Sam. "Well I guess not the way you walking around here singing and smiling all over the place, Myles done did a number on that personality," Michelle continued, "And if all the employees know it, so does Sam, but don't worry about him, he just mad cause you didn't give him a chance." "Girl, ain't nobody thinking about that man. Besides, you know I don't mess where I eat," Rhonda said as they both started to laugh.

"Sh, sh, you gone to get me in trouble. See that's why I'm a stop allowing you in my office," Rhonda said. "Girl, no you not, cause then who you going to *jone* with, and talk about Myles.....with," Michelle said jokingly. "Now, have you called him yet?" "Michelle, if you ask me that one more time! No, I haven't called him yet!" "Well what the heck is taking you so long?" she questioned. "I'm waiting until tonight when I get off work, so I won't be distracted, besides, I don't want to be interrupted by my pushy employees," she said as she rolled her eyes at Michelle.

"Don't you have work to do," Rhonda said demandingly with a laugh. "Oh, I'm going to go do my work, but you better be prepared with all the details tomorrow, Ms. Late night creepin," Michelle said, as she made her way to the doorway just as she finished speaking. "All the details too," she said as she continued down the hall. Rhonda sat in her office and laughed for a moment, then decided it was time to get back to work.

"Ami honey, dinner is ready," Rhonda said from the kitchen. "Here I come Mommy," Ami's sweet voice echoed from the hallway. "What are we having," she said as she positioned herself at the table. "Spaghetti and meatballs, honey," Rhonda said as she sat the dish on the table. "Did you finish all of your homework?" Rhonda asked Ami. "Most of it, I still have some math problems to do." "Ok, make sure I see them before you put them away," Rhonda continued to fix their plates.

"Well that's it, let's eat," she said. Rhonda sat for a moment contemplating how to talk to Ami about Myles, then finally she said, "Honey, you like Dr. Myles don't you?" "He's so nice mommy, why?" "Well, he asked me out Friday night. What do you think about that?" Rhonda asked as she looked at Ami from the corner of her eye. "It's about time! I thought he would never get around to asking. I told you that you liked him," Ami said with excitement. "So, where are we going?" "*We* are not going anywhere, young lady, just he and I are going out," Rhonda explained.

"Oh, well, that's ok, but wait. Where am I going" Ami asked with disappointment? "To your auntie Michelle's and Uncle Raymond's for the evening," Rhonda said as she laughed. "Well that is ok too. Me and my girls need to talk anyway," she said in her mature voice. "Ha! You and your 'girls'? Oh, y'all rollin' like that huh" Rhonda questioned as she began to laugh at Ami's demeanor?

She was growing up so fast and her wittiness was something else. "As long as he brings us our flowers this time, I'm ok with you going out with him," she said without hesitation. "Our flowers, it would be unusual for a man to bring a child and the mother flowers on the first date, Ami," said Rhonda a bit puzzled by the comment. "Well it's not the first time, now is it mommy?" Ami replied. "What do you mean, it's not the first time," Rhonda questioned? "He brought us flowers every day when we were at the hospital, one for you, and one for me, a different color every day," Ami said with a pronounced dictation to every word. "What? I thought, what?" Rhonda exclaimed. She was completely floored, and the expression on her face showed it.

"Now Mommy, you didn't know he brought them when he came to check on me. I even told you our flowers were there every day," Ami replied as if she was confused as to why Rhonda didn't know the flowers were from Dr. Myles. "What do you mean every day," Rhonda said in shock. "He would come and check on me every day to make sure we were ok, at first he told me not to say anything to you, but I thought you knew he was coming. After the first time, he left just before you came in the room." "No, I didn't know, I can't believe I never saw him, Rhonda said. "Well it's just like church then, you never saw him there either, but he was," Ami responded, as if it was no big deal.

Rhonda sat there pondering what all of this was about and tried to finish her food. She was so taken back with emotions she could hardly eat another bite. She sat through the remainder of the meal almost in complete silence, whereas this usually was the time she and Ami would talk about their day. When dinner was over, she decided she needed her weekly 'relax your mind' glass of wine. She could not wait until she saw Michelle to have one or two, beside she was going to need a bit of calming before she called Myles. Dinner seemed to drag on for some time, until Ami stood and said. "I'm done mommy, I'm going to finish my homework."

Picking up the phone after she poured herself a glass of wine, she drank half the glass. She realized all this time she had not saved Myles phone number. She walked to the bedroom and looked for the card and paperwork they had given her from Ami's ER visit when she heard her phone ringing in the living room. Realizing the only number on the forms was the one for the hospital and Myles card had the same number and his answering service number, she placed the papers back in the drawer and headed to the living room to answer her phone.

She picked up the phone and recognized the number calling which wasn't saved to her phone, it was Myles. She could not believe he was calling her when she was thinking about how to call him and she sure didn't want to ask Mrs. Johnson for the number. The least that women knew the better, she thought to herself.

"Hello," she said as she grabbed her glass of wine from the bookshelf. "Good evening Rhonda," the deep-toned voice said on the other line. "How are you this evening," Myles questioned? "I'm well. How about you?" "I'm doing fine at this moment," Myles replied, "I was hoping you had the chance to check your schedule. Are you free Friday evening?" "Yes, I have, and I am free. What time," Rhonda asked? "I was thinking I could pick you up around 6:00 that evening. Would that work for you?" "That would be fine," she said with a smile. "Great. Well how was your day? I'm sorry, were you busy? Do you have a moment to talk," he questioned as to not interrupt her evening plans. "No, I'm free at the moment, my day was somewhat comical to say the least about it."

"Oh, really, how was it comical," Myles asked. "Well, let's just say, I am learning to walk in the sun and it's noticeable," "Oh, I see," Myles said as he chuckled a bit, "How is my girl, Ami?" "She is fine, she's doing her homework right now, and speaking of Ami," Rhonda said with a pause, "she told me you checked on her every day when she was at the hospital and brought her flowers. Is that true?" "Well, she wasn't supposed to say anything, but yes this is true, and for the record, I was checking on both of you and the flowers were also for the two of you," Myles explained. "Well, I was just wondering why you didn't say anything or come when I was there, is all," she said.

"Well, would you have welcomed my visit at the time? I just believed you were not ready for the type of attention I was ready to give you, and I wanted to make sure you both were ok," Myles continued. "I guess I was a bit standoffish, wasn't I," Rhonda said in a joking tone. "A little," Myles said. "You went from beside me, to the back of the room in the ER, so I wasn't about to set myself up for you moving to the other side of the city at that point. Besides, I knew God would bring you back my way somehow," "What? Wow, so you knew this, huh?" Rhonda questioned. "Well, is that why you never said anything at the church, because Ami also told me you come every Sunday?" "That is exactly why, I didn't want you to feel uncomfortable in any way, I can tell when a woman has been through something and may not be ready for where I'm trying to go, and I'm patient enough to allow you to get ready for me," he said.

Rhonda was now speechless and overwhelmed by the words Myles spoke to her. "So, what is it or where is it you want to go with me," She questioned? "Well, I would rather you and I take the time to get to know each other and that way I can show you better than I can tell you," he replied. "Oh, is that right," she said. Now, feeling assured Myles was about action and not the type of guy she had normally been approached by, she felt more confident in her desires to spend time with him.

As they talked a little longer about the type of date he would be taking her on, she started to understand Myles was not the type of man to play mind games nor was he the type of man who she would be able to withhold any information about her life and past from. The question now was when and how she would tell him of her past.

After some time on the phone with Myles, she started to feel herself really relax with him. Their conversations seemed to flow so smoothly. It was as if they had been knowing each other for years. Finding they had a lot in common made it easy for Rhonda to be open and truly be herself on the phone with him. This was easy. Suddenly Rhonda started to feel the way she had felt the day before when she was on the phone with Michelle.

The feeling of fear started to overtake her. She knew at this point it had nothing to do with Myles, because this wasn't the first time, she had felt this way. Myles picked up on her silence and said, "Ok, where did you go? Am I wearing you out already with all this conversation?" "No, it's just been a long day," Rhonda said as she tried to pull herself back to the conversation and let go of what she was feeling.

As the evening progressed, she felt it was time to check on Ami and make sure she was getting ready for bed. "Well, Myles, I have enjoyed speaking with you, but I have to check on Ami." "It's has been such a pleasure speaking with you as well and I look forward to seeing you on Friday at 6 o'clock," Myles said. "Ok, sounds good, goodnight Myles," Rhonda said as she stood to take her wine glass in the kitchen. "Good night Rhonda," Myles said as they both hang up.

Rhonda made her way to the kitchen and found herself finishing the dinner dishes she had left. She stood over the sink replaying the conversation in her head she had just had with Myles. There was something so different about this man, and she found it so easy to respect him, because she didn't feel he was attracted to her appearance alone. Thinking to herself about some of the other men who had approached her and the types of conversations they would have just in passing.

Most of the men she had come in contact with in the past, before Myles, let her know from the start they wanted something more than just friendship from her, by the words they would say about her skin or her hair and how soft she looked. All of these had been red flags from the start, but the things Myles did to check on her and Ami and standing back for so long making sure she was ready to receive him, made her feel more sure that he was a respectable person and desired to be her friend.

Besides, any man with a mother like Mrs. Johnson had to have some true morals about themselves, because she wouldn't stand for anything else. Rhonda laughed to herself as she thought about what Myles's childhood must have been like with Mrs. Johnson as his mother. That man probably couldn't get away with nothing! She laughed as she finished up and put the leftovers away.

Making her way down the hall to check in on Ami, she entered the doorway to peep in. Ami had taken her shower and placed her homework on the dresser for Rhonda to check. Rhonda saw Ami sitting up in the bed with, *The Message* upright in her lap." "Hey sweetie, you already for bed?" Ami looking up at Rhonda, "Yes, Mommy, my homework is over there and I'm just reading." "Ok baby," Rhonda said as she picked up the paper and began to review it, "looks good baby, I'm going to get myself ready for bed too, don't stay up to long, ok," she said as she placed the paper back on the dresser and pulled the door together, leaving just a slight crack. "Ok," Ami replied as she quickly dropped her head back down, eyes glued to the words leaping off the page to her, she was so excited and didn't want to take away from the excitement, she was getting to the good part.

Rhonda now excited about her date with Myles, turned on the shower and retreated to her room where she continued to ponder on all the things Myles had done in secret to ensure Ami and she were ok. She could not help but smile, this was the most attention she'd had in a long time if ever and it was starting to feel really good. She still did not know why the feeling of fear kept sweeping over her, so she decided she would do something she had not done a lot of since she gave her life to God, she was going to pray.

She finished her shower and kneeled to the side of the bed. She knew and trusted God at this point enough to know he would help her overcome her fears, or at the very least help her understand why she was having these feeling more often. With everything happening in her life, she could not assume it was just her imagination, not when she was trying so hard to move forward and be happy walking in the sun.

PEEPING CHESTER

"Have you seen the new tenant yet," Rhonda heard as she was checking the mail. It was Mrs. Johnson standing in the doorway, loud whispering, down the hall. Rhonda looked around to see if she was the only one in the hallway, realizing that she was talking to her. She closed the mailbox and walked towards Mrs. Johnson. "No, Mrs. Johnson and I haven't been looking for them either," Rhonda said sarcastically. "Well it's not a them it's a him, and it seems to me he be looking for you, the way he is always speaking to Ami when she comes in here."

"What," Rhonda asked as she fixed her bag and placed the mail inside? "Well he can keep looking cause I'm not interested." "Well good because I don't like the way he always goes to check his mail when that bus pulls up, it's like he is waiting for Ami to come in, looking towards the door. He seems like a creeper to me. Maybe you should have a talk with Ami about not talking to him," Mrs. Johnson said. "Every new friend ain't always a good friend, plus he makes sure he sees when you come home too."

"I'm not even going to ask how you know any of this," Rhonda said as she turned to walk away. "Ok, Mrs. Johnson, I will definitely speak to her and find out what he is saying, I'm sure it's nothing, Ami is usually very careful not to talk to strangers or linger around she knows to get inside and lock the door." "I know she does, but it's just something about this man, the way he talks to her is strange, just be careful is all I'm saying," Mrs. Johnson concluded with passion. "Ok, thank you for watching out for us, it really means a lot." "I hope so because some people call me Nosey, but I just know how the devil operates," she said as she closed the door and began the process of locking her locks.

Rhonda laughed to herself at the last comment Mrs. Johnson made, knowing she was one of the people who called her Mrs. Nosey. She made her way up the stairs to her apartment, where she found Ami seated at the dining room table. "Hey baby," Rhonda said as she made her way to the kitchen and placed her bag on the counter. "Sorry, I ran a little late, had to stop and get some milk and eggs for the morning. How are you baby, how was your day?"

"It was good, I just don't have any friends here anymore," Ami said with tears in her eyes. "What do you mean, Ami," Rhonda questioned as she walked over to Ami placing her arm around her shoulders? "Kianna went to be with Jesus and left me here." Ami said as she burst into tears, "You should have let her live with us, if she could have just stayed for a little while," she shouted through the tears.

Rhonda, not knowing what was going on grabbed Ami and hugged her tight.

The phone rang and Ami sat up in the chair trying to get herself together. "Hello," Rhonda said as she tried to pull herself away from Ami. "Hello, Ms. Hodge, this is Mrs. Valier, the school counselor, how are you this evening?" "I am fine and you?" Rhonda said as she was trying to wrap her mind around what Ami had just told her. Still confused, "How may I help you, Rhonda asked as she continued to look at Ami and make sure she was alright? "Well, I'm calling with some very sad news. It seems one of our students lost their life last night in a domestic violence situation, and we are now calling parents to let them know, in hopes they would talk to their child and comfort them as we try and work through the details, case by case with the students."

"We wanted to make sure you knew how close Ami and the young lady Kianna were. It would seem they spent every afternoon together on the playground and Ami knew the situation this young child was facing every day when she went home. We know this because we had a brief talk with Ami when we found out who her friends were." She continued, "The strangest part of this, was when we went to inform Ami she already knew and she in fact told us before we could tell her and also told us she had talked to her on the playground that morning."

"Now, we have no clue as to why Ami would say these things, because Kianna passed away in the wee hours of the morning, but Ami is a very special young lady and we know she would never fabricate something of this magnitude." "We are just wanting you both to know if there is anything we can do or that you need, we are here for her and you," she continued.

"Oh, my goodness, I am so sorry to hear this, I was wondering what was going on with her tonight, thank you so much for letting me know. I will speak with Ami now and let you know if we need anything," Rhonda said as she rubbed Ami's back. "Thank you again for calling,"

"You are welcome, we will be letting the parents know of any funeral arrangements for Kianna in a few days. Thanks for your time," she said. "Ami is in my thoughts and prayers as well as this family. Have a good evening," she concluded. "Thank you, so much and our prayers are with the family too," Rhonda said as she hung up the phone. "Ami, baby I am so sorry this has happened," Rhonda exclaimed as she kneeled beside the chair Ami was sitting in. "I know you are hurting and that's ok, do you want to talk about it, sweetie," Rhonda almost in tears seeing Ami so broken. "No, I just want my friend," Ami said as she sobbed into Rhonda's shoulder. "I know baby, I know," Rhonda said compassionately as she held Ami tighter and just allowed her to cry until she had no more tears.

Rhonda finally got Ami off to bed after a long hot soak in the tub and a cup of her mother's home-made hot chocolate. She sat on the couch emotionally exhausted, for a few minutes to get herself together. She couldn't shake the image of Ami crying so hard. She had had moments with Ami when she was upset but never like this and never anything close to the death of her closest friend. Someone she clearly loved very much, so much so that she wanted to protect her.

As she sat thinking, she thought about how much she wanted to protect Ami even more from anything that could hurt her this deeply, but she realized there was nothing she could do to protect her from matters of the heart, no more than she could protect herself. Rhonda could not help but wonder about Myles and how much Ami liked him.

She began to think to herself how things would play out for Ami if this did not work out, hoping a father was not something Ami was betting on. As she sat there thinking, she let the conversation with Mrs. Johnson completely slip her mind. She'd forgotten to ask Ami about the man and what he had said to her. All she could think of was how broken-hearted Ami was about her friend's death and wonder if it was a mistake to get involved with Myles. Would her chance to walk in the sun only last for a moment and end up costing her and Ami more heartache in the long run. This was something she would have to keep in her mind she thought, "I can't go losing myself in this too fast, I will just be cautious."

The next morning, Rhonda went in to wake Ami, only to find her sitting on the edge of the bed in tears. She knew this was going to be hard on her, "Good Morning, baby. I know this is hard and it will be hard for some time. You have to understand death is a part of life, we will all die one day. It's the living that is hard, because you have to live without that person. Just know that she is safe now, she is ok and you living your best life will make her so happy." Rhonda said as she kneeled beside Ami to comfort her. "I know Mommy, I was just praying for her father, that he would get help and forgive himself, because she doesn't hurt anymore, but I know this will be hard for him to live with." Rhonda in shock, began to tear up. She could not believe what Ami was saying. "Sometimes the hardest thing is to forgive yourself when you have done something so terrible, but God will forgive him if he asks Him to," Ami said as she wiped her tears and gave Rhonda a hug.

Rhonda knew in that moment Ami had learned Mercy and she had learned it completely. "I'm going to get ready for school now Mommy, I'm ok," Ami said as she released her hold on Rhonda. "Ohhhhkay, you sure you want to go today, with all that has happened?" she questioned. "Oh, yeah, living my best life didn't start today, it's been going on, I just have to learn to live it without my friend and I have to start that today," Ami said. "Well alright then," Rhonda replied as she stood to her feet. "You are too mature for a nine-year-old," Rhonda said. "Yeah, but not for a ten-year-old," Ami said as they both laughed. "You still have another week before all of this happens, and if nine is any indication of what to expect at ten, then Lord help me."

As they rode to before care, Rhonda decided to ask Ami

about Myles. "Ami what do you think about Myles?" "He's great. Why," Ami replied as she looked at her papers? "Well I was just wondering if it would be too much for him to be a part of our lives right now, what if he didn't stay in our lives for long," Rhonda asked hesitantly? "Well Mommy, I think you should live your best life too and if Dr. Myles is going to help you live it, then I think you should give it a chance."

Rhonda, now speechless continued to drive looking straight ahead amazed at Ami's response. "Well I guess you have a point again, when did you get so wise little girl?" "Well, I have been holding back, you see, but I think it's a gift, you know like what *The Message* talks about," Ami said as she acted as if it was no big deal. "Well I needed that gift many years ago, and you seem to operate in it very well," Rhonda said with wide eyes.

Rhonda continued to think about what Ami had said, and knew she was right. It was time for her to live in the life God had blessed her with, after all she had been through. It was time for her to stop just living day to day but to thrive and shoot for her best life - open herself up to new experiences and opportunities, find her light and walk in it. She smiled to herself. Myles could be the one who is going to help her live her best life in this season. There was something about the way he brought out her inter beauty in just a few conversations.

She was beginning to feel as if no man had ever touched her so deeply with such thoughtfulness in not just his words but his actions as well. Myles was definingly a man of action, but he wasn't pushy, and he didn't try to force his way in. She couldn't help but see God, because he had all the attributes thus far, of the way God dealt with her, and Myles's fine tail was definitely a gift from God to this world, she thought as she chuckled a bit to herself.

"What Mommy," Ami questioned as she continued to read her paper? "Oh, nothing baby, just thinking to myself," Rhonda replied. "Oh, Mrs. Allen always tells us don't think too long, you must know therefore you must study." "Well Ami baby this is a kind of study for grown folks and when you're older you will do it too and sometimes you will laugh to yourself too," Rhonda said, "Just make sure you're around people you trust when you do or someone may think your nuts!" "Yeah, I try not to think that too often about you, because you do it a lot," Ami said with a giggle. "Oh yeah, I'm going to see if I'm nuts when that birthday comes next week too, while ya talkin' smack," Rhonda replied as they both laughed out loud. "You're not serious, though. Right?" Ami asked sharply.

Rhonda ignored Ami's last comment and went back to her thoughts while she continued to drive. She knew this could be something special with Myles because she felt safe when she saw or talked to him - even more special than how James and she started out all those years ago, before everything went so terribly wrong. She thought back on the time she and James were together in college. He always made sure she felt comfortable around him and his friends, no matter how boyish they were being. He never missed a special moment and made sure he spent his last on some type of gift to celebrate the occasion.

She began to reminisce on the day James went to meet her family, he was very nervous, wondering if they would except him. She encouraged him, knowing that he had a lot to offer and so many dreams and aspirations. James made the mistake of sharing some of his dreams with Rhonda's mother. All she could think was how she knew that was the worst thing he could have done, but she also knew her mother had a way of bringing out what's in you. Rhonda remembered how her mother looked at him and couldn't help but laugh, she looked at him as though he was blowing smoke, and she knew James enough to know, he would set out to prove everyone who had doubted him wrong.

Rhonda was sure that moment was the turning point for James. James had suffered many pains in his past from his father not being in his life. He doubted he was able to be a man in a sense, always looking for someone to affirm him in everything he did and when he didn't get it from those he sought it from he made sure he showed them how much of a man he could be. She knew also, one of the reasons he entered the relationship with his partner, was because he affirmed his manhood like a father. There was nothing this man didn't do to pull James in and when he finally convinced him to come on board, things from that moment started to go south.

As she pulled up to before care to drop Ami off, she

decided she wasn't going to think about those things anymore. That was a past she would never see again, and she was over it. She was going to do what Ami had suggested and that was to allow herself to live her best life, and if that included Myles, she was willing to give it all she had.

Rhonda entered the before care building. Mrs. Williams was surprised to see her enter, and greeted Ami. "Well what do I owe the pleasure of this surprise," Mrs. Williams said sarcastically to Rhonda. "I was wondering if I could speak to you in private for a moment," Rhonda said with a seriousness in her tone. "Yes, Dear. What seems to be the trouble," she said as she stepped into the hallway, pulling the door together. Rhonda began to explain all the events which had occurred as she knew them, thus far. As she spoke with Mrs. Williams, she informed her she did not know all the details surrounding the death of Kiana. She then began to explain to her, Ami seemed to be fine, but she was not sure. She wasn't expressing grief in another way.

Rhonda gave her as many details about the situation as she could and told her of how Ami prayed for the father that morning and how she felt it was her way of handling her grief. Mrs. Williams didn't bother to give Rhonda any of her usual sarcastic comments knowing this was a serious time. she promised to keep an eye on Ami and make sure to let her know if she saw any signs Ami was not adjusting to the loss of her best friend.

Rhonda went on to work where she knew she would talk to Michelle about what she was feeling and get advice on how to handle the situation with Ami. The last thing she needed was to try and handle this on her own, she needed her friend. This was new to her and she knew she needed to handle it with care. She knew Michelle was wise and even if she had never experienced it before she would listen and even cry with her if she needed her to.

Rhonda pulled up to the parking lot and seeing Michelle getting out of her car, she parked the car and gathered her things. Michelle was there waiting by her car, she had spotted Rhonda pulling in. "Hey girl, good morning," Michelle said groggy from morning. "How are you girl," Michelle continued as she fixed her purse on her shoulder? "Girl, tired, it's been a long night," Rhonda said with a sigh. "Long night, that doesn't sound good at all, what's going on girl," Michelle asked with concern? "Girl, the school called." Michelle interrupted, "I know you not 'bout to tell me my baby got in trouble, because they are lying!" "Girl no, will you hush and let me tell you," Rhonda said as she giggled. "OK, well let me backtrack, when I got home yesterday Ami, was sitting at the table crying." "Did somebody hurt her, I'm going up there," Michelle said with fight in her voice. "Girl if you don't hush, and let me tell you what happened, before we have to go in this place, I need to get this out," Rhonda was still giggling at Michelle's protectiveness of Ami. She knew when it came to Ami and *them girls*, she didn't play.

Rhonda was now gaining Michelle's full attention and hesitantly continued as if to say "are you going to be quiet now?" "Then," pausing for a moment to make sure Michelle was not going to interrupt, "the school called, and the counselor told me that one of the little girls Ami talks to every day had been involved in a domestic violence issue." "Oh My Goodness," Michelle said in shock! "Apparently she died," Michelle now in complete shock "What! Are you serious?" "Yes!" Rhonda said, "Ami was so shook-up, I didn't know what to say or do, turns out this little girl was Ami's best friend."

"I mean she had always talked about her and every time I would invite her over for a play date the mother would say no." "I never really thought much of it, because I wasn't about to let Ami spend the night anywhere other than your house either, so..." Rhonda said as she shrugged her shoulders. "Oh my goodness, I know that baby is hurting," Michelle said with concern. "Michelle that's just it, the counselor said Ami knew about the little girl being deceased." "What do you mean, she knew," Michelle asked. "The counselor told me, Ami said she talked to Kianna that morning on the playground and I got the feeling she believed Ami, because she also told me Ami was a special little girl and would never lie. But the counselor said she died the night before."

"I'm having so much trouble figuring this thing out with Ami." "It is like she knows things, like before they happen or she says thing a child her age couldn't possibly know.

You know what I mean, Michelle," Rhonda pondered with light frustration? "Well, it sounds to me like Ami is prophetic, and she may be able to speak to those who have passed on that she is connected to before they ascend to heaven" Michelle replied. "What do you mean prophetic, and what, talking to dead people," Rhonda exclaimed, completely puzzled?" "Like in the olden days, girl you know, the gifts they have in the Bible," Michelle explained. "Okay, now you know the scripture that goes, auhh, He gave some apostles, some prophets, some teachers, some evangelist, right, well He didn't stop giving those gifts, and that's what it sounds like Ami has, a gift, and a few of them to boot," Michelle said as if to even question it herself.

"Maybe so, but I just hope she doesn't feel sad all the time now, because she and that little girl were so close. All she kept saying to me was that if I had let her come and live with us for a little while, she would have been ok. And I pray she doesn't blame me somehow. I don't know why she didn't tell me this little girl was being abused. The counselor said she would call or send something home with more details about the situation and funeral."

Rhonda felt better after talking about things with Michelle. Michelle looked at her phone and said, "We're going to have to go to her funeral and pay our respects and I think that will be good closure". "I think that would be good for Ami," Rhonda replied. Michelle said, "What, I'm talking about you too." Rhonda laughed and said "You're not just going to get out of this one with a talk, Godparents support their Godchildren and you goin', matter of fact, the whole family goin'," Rhonda said as they both laughed and turn towards the entrance of the restaurant.

"How you just gon' make us all have to go? My soul can't handle the death of a child! I'm not feeling that in my shannnanna…" Michelle said as they continued to walk and laugh. "Have you heard from Myles," Michelle casually interrupted the laughter. "Girl, not since the other night," Rhonda replied. Michelle looked with surprise, as Rhonda spoke, "So when is the date," Michelle asked? "Well it's Friday," Rhonda said nervously as she continued. "I'm not sure if I should go, I think maybe Ami needs me more right now," Rhonda said. "Awe naw, you're going on this date! We fought too hard and too long for this, Ami will be just fine with the girls, at my house," Michelle demanded. "The question now is, do we need an exit plan, are you gonna be ok in the company of Mr. Fine, I mean, with Myles on your own?" "I think I'll be fine. Besides, we have a lot in common, it seems. Girl, he likes all the food I like, all of my favorite movies, he even likes some of the girly ones," Rhonda said with excitement.

"Sounds like you're really into Mr. Myles, the way you talk and just smiling all big all the time, this could be something, huh" Michelle questioned. "I'm just glad you're taking a chance," "Michelle said laughing. "I know, girl after what Ami said this morning, I have no choice!" What, what do you mean, what did she say girl?" Michelle asked. "Ami told me Myles could be the one to help me live my best life!" "What!" "Girl, Ami must have really been trippin', but she might be onto something."

As they entered the building Rhonda told Michelle she would talk to her later, realizing it was getting late and she had to get some things done in her office. Michelle went to the floor to make sure the other workers arrived on schedule. The day passed by quickly. Rhonda had very little time to think about anything other than work, except the occasional thought of Ami, wondering if she was ok at school, and, of course, Myles.

As she pulled up to the apartment complex, she gathered all of her things from the car and headed towards the door. Approaching the sidewalk, she noticed a man standing at the mailbox, she concluded this was the man Mrs. Johnson had been talking about. There he stood about six feet three inches, with long dreads, a very lean, muscular physique, wearing a white tank top and jeans. Although his face was to the side, she felt uneasy, in fact, she noticed she was feeling the fear she had been feeling off and on lately, except this time it was directed towards a person and not a conversation.

Feeling it strange this man somewhat put her in the mind of someone familiar, she began her ascent, approaching the stairs. He must have turned when she was looking down to see the steps approaching and as she pulled the door open, he made his way through his door and stepped into his apartment closing the door. She thought she had a moment before he would shut the door, thinking this would be an opportunity to see who Ami had been speaking with.

Realizing she had too many things in her hands to take the opportunity and knock on the door, she continued up the stairs. While walking up the stairs she started thinking to herself, he's kind of built like James when we were in college." She managed to shake the thought off , summing it up with another thought, "James would never have dreadlocks, and he is much thinner than James cared to be, and built too." Rhonda open the door to the apartment and yelled for Ami, "Ami, baby I'm home!" "Hey Mommy, I'm in my room," she heard Ami reply from a distance. "OK, I'm going to start dinner."

LIVING OUT LOUD

All day Friday, Rhonda had been thinking about Myles, the date they would have this evening and all the phone conversations. She couldn't wait to get home, get dressed to go and meet him, but first she had to drop Ami off at Michelle's. Pulling up to Michelle's house she saw Michelle standing outside, "Hey girl. Come on, Ami. And you step out of that car right now and let me get a look at you from head to toe," Michelle said as Rhonda exited the car.

"Oh, shoot Miss Rhonda Hodge!" Woo, look at you girl. That man is going to drop to his knees," said Michelle as she looked Rhonda up and down. "Girl, hush, this just a little *somethin'* I threw on," Rhonda expressed as she rubbed down her waist and hips. "Hum, looks like you did more than just throw it on. Looks like you plastered it with a paint brush!" "Honey that dress is tight," Michelle said with a laugh. Rhonda fanned her away with her hand, "It is not! I have room to move. "Myles ain't going to be able to move, you gone give that man a heart attack! Yup, he going to be laying up in the very hospital where he works," Michelle teased.

"Hush, I got to go", Rhonda said with haste as she sat back in the car and positioned herself. "You sure you don't want to drive one of our cars?" "No, this man is going to get whatever comes with the package, including my old rusty," Rhonda said with conviction. "If you say so, but old rusty might just be a deal breaker," Michelle continued to tease. "OK, do we need a safety word, because he might be something totally different after he see that canvas you painted with that dress," Michelle said laughing her way through.

"Oh, you're just so funny this evening aren't you. No, I'll be fine, I'll text you when I get there," Rhonda said as she closed the car door. "OK, but don't be texting me throughout dinner. Pay attention to Myles, because Lord knows he's gonna be paying attention to you in that dress!" "OK, I will, I mean I won't." Rhonda said as she closed the window continuing to position herself, checking her makeup and lipstick. "Hey!" Michelle yelled at Rhonda's window, where are you guys going"? "We're meeting at a fancy restaurant in Shortsville, *The Rise.*" "Oh, yeah, that's like 10 minutes from here," Michelle questioned? "Uh huh, it is. I know," Rhonda said as she put the car in reverse, pulled out of the driveway, excited she was going to see Myles. "Make sure you have fun and be safe," Michelle yelled, as Rhonda rolled the window all the way up and drove away.

Rhonda pulled around in front of the restaurant and exited the car, handing the valet her keys to park her car. Feeling a bit bad she had to give instructions on how to jimmy the door to enter her old rusty vehicle. At that moment she was really feeling like she needed a new car. Walking up to the restaurant doors, she hoped not to find Myles standing there. She had no idea if he had seen her hooptie yet and she didn't want tonight to be the first time he did. Breathing a sigh of relief, she looked in the doorway and didn't see Myles, hoping he was not running late.

She felt her phone buzz in her purse. Reaching to grab it, she saw she'd received a message, "I'm over in the corner," It was Myles. Rhonda replied with a smile emoji as she headed in his direction. She hoped she was looking OK and that her dress really wasn't as tight as Michelle made it out to be. Fixing her dress, as she approached the table Myles stood up smiling as though he had seen an angel for the first time. Rhonda had truly taken his breath in that moment. He could hardly speak as he walked over to greet her, pulling out her chair. He knew that she was beautiful, but he had no idea she was *this* beautiful.

Pausing for a moment to compose himself, he managed to speak, "Hello, Beautiful," he whispered softly in her ear. Myles said this with a kiddush nervousness and reached his arms around her to hug her. Rhonda replied with the same nervousness, "Hello, thank you, and how are you?" "I'm fine," Myles said as he let her go, turning to pull her seat out from the table. He waited for a moment as she positioned herself and pushed her chair, still admiring her attire and elegance. Myles unable to take his eyes off her, returned to his seat and stared at her for a moment, "You are truly breath taking!" Rhonda wasn't familiar with this type of attention from a man without it feeling explicit and she settled in, feeling more than comfortable. "Thank you," she smiled softly.

"You look very handsome yourself." Myles smiled and grabbed Rhonda's hand from across the table. "Thank you. I guess we make a nice pair." "I guess we do," Rhonda replied. She couldn't believe she was being so honest and open. "How was your day?" Myles asked as he grabbed the wine menu and placed it to the side. "Oh, I'm going to need a glass of that," Rhonda said as she chuckled. "Oh, really?" Myles said, "I knew you would, so I've already ordered a couple of glasses." "I hope you like what I selected, I'm not much of a drinker but you can have as much as you like." "I would hope you're not trying to get me tipsy," Rhonda said with a slightly serious look on her face. "Never that, if you did get tipsy, I would never take advantage," Myles said as he smiled at her. Suddenly his look became serious and he said, "Sober Rhonda is who I want."

Rhonda now her breath was taken by his comment and she picked up the menu and begin to peruse it. "My day was ok, how was your day," she questioned as if to change the subject quickly? Trying not to look at him to see if it worked, she felt him continue to stare at her. She, lifting her head making eye contact, noticed he had this look on his face she had never seen. "My day was wonderful, I spent the whole day pondering what this night would be like," he said managing not to take his eyes off her for a moment. Rhonda thought to herself, "Wow!"

She could not believe how honest he was being, yet, managing to be such a gentleman in the way and the things he said. Most men would not come out and say that they're not going to take advantage. There was a moment of silence and the waiter stepped over to the table with two glasses of wine. They paused from their silent glares to notice the waiter. Rhonda touched the glass as he sat it on the table, insuring it was steadied. "Please, let me know when you're ready to order," he said as he took a step back from the table, pausing for a reply. "OK, thank you, give us just a minute or two." "No problem Sir," the waiter said as he turned and walked to the other side of the floor.

They sat sipping the wine for several minutes. Rhonda tasted it several times, "This is wonderful." "I thought you might like it. I'll have to remember this selection for our special occasions," Myles said as he smiled at her. "What do you mean, *our special occasions*, this is our first real date," Rhonda said with a confused giggle. "I hope it won't be the last," Myles replied softly. "Maybe not, if you play your cards right, it won't," Rhonda said sarcastically.

"I heard that. Just don't go stand in the corner," Myles said jokingly, "You know how you like to do, just stand on the other side of the atmosphere, I mean, just shut completely down." "I won't, I'm going to remain very present, I promise," laughing out loud. She couldn't believe he went there, "Don't come for me." "Too late, I had to, I'm going to use that one a lot," he said as they both laughed. "I cannot believe you went there; however, it is rather funny, when you think about it," Rhonda said as she reached for her glass.

The evening progressed somehow. Time was flying – yet stood still. Rhonda and Myles talked about everything they could think of, everything except Rhonda's past. "So, did you know I lived in the building with your mother," Rhonda said. "Yes, I have to admit I did. I knew, I just never thought you would be friends with my mother," Myles answered with a laugh. "I know for myself; she can be very nosey, and I didn't think that you would befriend someone who was all in your business. I mean, just look how you shut me down from the start." Laughing Rhonda interjected, "Yes, Mrs. Johnson can be nosey, but after you get to know her, she is still nosey. No, but seriously, she's sweet and I've grown to love her."

"I'm hoping you'll love her a lot more," Myles said as he took a sip of his wine. "Listen…, I know, well she makes it hard sometimes," Rhonda said, as they both laughed. Myles agreed as he nodded his head up and down. "Yes, she sure can, even for her son," he said with raised brows. They both continued to laugh even more. "Your mom is a very genuine person, and she has blessed us so much in such a short time," Rhonda said. "Like the way she was watching out for Ami when I couldn't make it straight home, but she never let on." "I mean, come to find out, she's been doing it this whole time, even before I met her," Rhonda said a little teary eyed. "Wow, yes, my mother is a caregiver and even more compassionate than she lets on," Myles said, realizing the bond between the two.

"Where do your parents live?" Myles asked abruptly. "Oh, they live down South," Rhonda said nervously. She was unsure how much at this point to reveal to Myles about her life before she came here. "Yeah, where exactly in the south," he began to question. "I'm not sure you have ever heard of it, it's not a big city but big things happen down south, a place called Monroe Ville, Texas," Rhonda said with hesitance. "Oh, where exactly is that, I'd love to visit one day" Myles questioned? "Well, we will have to see about that. Let's, just get through the first date," Rhonda replied jokingly.

Looking at Myles's eagerness to know more, she knew this was not the time to spill her tea. "OK," Myles said with a laugh, "I'll take that. I don't want to get ahead of myself. I have to make sure you don't run," he said sarcastically. "Besides, I can tell this is a touchy subject already and I can tell you don't share lightly," Myles picked up on her vibes. "True, no I don't," she said as she took another sip of her wine then a bite of her food. Myles said assertively, "The last thing I need you to do is run from me now, no matter how good the conversation has been." Rhonda smiled, thankful for the conclusion of the line of questioning, shocked at how well Myles seemed to know her, she could feel her heart skip a beat.

When dinner was complete, they sat talking for another 30 minutes, talking about work and the people they spent time with. Rhonda not having very many people she entertained as friends, found herself very limited in the conversation. Myles took the lead, trying to ensure she remained comfortable with him and ensure that he was not prying. "What are you and Ami doing this weekend? I would love to hang out with the two of you?" Myles asked, hoping he wasn't too eager. "I have to take Ami to a funeral tomorrow," Rhonda said with sadness on her face. "Take her to a funeral? Was it a family member...," he asked completely shocked and concerned?

"Who passed away?" he continued to ask with a look of compassion. Rhonda had only experienced this look for a moment in the hospital, but she knew from that experience Myles was very concerned. "Ami's best friend for the last few years. She was involved in domestic violence," Rhonda said, tears filling her eyes. "Her father murdered her. We don't really know all the details, the school just sent a letter home with the details of the service." "Oh, my goodness, I'm sorry to hear that," Myles said as he rubbed his bald head, "that's terrible, is there anything I can do?" "No, Ami just needs time to grieve and I'm not too sure she is doing that very well. If you could just pray for us both," Rhonda said as her grief began to explode into tears. "Oh, don't cry sweetheart, I already pray for you both, and if it's not too much trouble," Myles interjected, "I'd like to be there for her and support her and you."

Rhonda now in shock, "What?," she said with a tremble in her voice, "you want to come to the funeral, really?" "Listen," Myles said, "I'm not just here to be a part of your life, date you and not take the time to share in the hard things. I want to be a part of Ami's life, also." "What kind of man would I be if I didn't share in all of it or want to know about all of it? I want to support her and you in any way I can, as a friend," he said. "Oh wow, what you've never had a man support you," He questioned? "Well not like this," Rhonda said questionably. "Well, get used to it, this is who I am," Myles said with a serious tone. Rhonda could tell he meant every word, but she expected nothing less given the mother he had. "Now, can I come to the funeral or not," he asked, with a smile?

Rhonda, still somewhat in shock, "Yes, I think Ami would appreciate that." "Ok, is it alright for me to pick you guys up," Myles asked? "Yes, that would be fine," she said clearing her throat. "What time will you be ready," he asked her. "We'll be ready about 10:30," Rhonda said. "OK, I'll be there," Myles said sitting back in his chair. He hated for the night to end, but he knew he had to move somethings around for him to be able to pick them up and he was more than willing.

"Well, it looks like everybody is leaving but us. Are you ready to go," Rhonda asked? "No, not really, but I guess I do get to see you in the morning," Myles said with a smile. "Don't be fresh," Rhonda said sharply, as they both laughed. "I'm not," Myles said as he continued to smile and laugh. "It just happened to come out that way," he said still laughing to himself. "Yeah, Ok," Rhonda said, as she stood from the table and grabbed her purse. "I'll walk you out," Myles said as he quickly stood from the table. "That's ok, I'll find my way and see you tomorrow," Rhonda said quickly, reaching for a hug goodbye. "OK," Myles said as he began to embrace her tightly, "I'll get the check."

Rhonda now feeling as though she didn't want the night to end, realized it really was getting late and she knew Michelle was waiting up. She turned to walk away she could feel Myles watching her. He was standing as though he couldn't move until she was no longer seen. She was just hoping he didn't follow her, because she did not want him to see her get into her car. Rhonda gave the valet her ticket and he ran to get her car. She stood there waiting, hoping Myles didn't come out the door behind her.

As the valet pulled up, she breathed a sigh of relief and walked around to get in the car. The valet held the door open for her, slamming the door extra hard as he did not forget her previous instructions when she had arrived. Rhonda sat in the seat and breathed deeply, then she exhaled. This night was amazing, and she felt so surreal, as if she was floating on a cloud. Now she had to focus on the road and make it to Michelle's house to pick up Ami.

"Hello? Michelle answered. "Hey Sis!" Rhonda said as she continued with a giggle. "Ouuugghhh sounds like someone had a nice time," Michelle replied. "Girl, I have to admit this man is like none I have ever met or at least in a very long time!" Rhonda said with excitement. "I mean, and girl why is he going to the funeral to support Ami tomorrow!" "I'm just blown away!" "I can tell," Michelle interrupted, "I also know tonight is not the night to get the details. You are just too overwhelmed by tonight, you couldn't possibly stay on track with my details." "Your details," Rhonda asked in shock? "Yes, now you know how I love my details, so I'm going to need you to keep a lid on it until Sunday at Ami's birthday party, cause we are going to need that as a filler, with all these kids," Michelle said. "Ha ha, very funny, I guess you're right though," said Rhonda as they both laughed. "I take it you're on your way?" Michelle questioned. "Yeah, I am," "Good I didn't want to have to come looking for you, so get ya' fast tail on over here," Michelle said sarcastically.

A little while after picking Ami up from Michelle's and getting settled in for the night, Rhonda rushed to her ringing phone. "Hello, I hope it's not too late. I just wanted to make sure you made it home safely." Myles asked with a longing in his voice. "Well, hello. We did," Rhonda said softly. "I really had a wonderful time tonight," she said. "I did too," Myles replied. "You know it is getting rather late, I think maybe we should talk tomorrow," Rhonda said. "That sounds wonderful, I'll see you in the morning, then," Myles said. "OK, good, night. "Good night," Myles said as they both hang-up.

****

"Ami are you ready honey?" Rhonda yelled down the hall. "Yes, mommy," Ami's sweet voice rang out from the hallway. Rhonda could tell she was sad and trying to be upbeat. "I'm ready too, Myles will be here any minute," Rhonda said. "I know mommy, I'm ready, here I come," Ami said as she walked down the hall. Rhonda looked around for her keys and heard her phone ringing in the other room. She headed to answer it, "Hello." "Good morning beautiful, how are you and Ami this morning," the deep voice said on the other end. "We're Ok, I'm just trying to keep my eyes on Ami and make sure she's Ok," Rhonda explained. "Well I plan to keep my eyes on both of you, are you ready," Myles asked. "Yes, just heading out the door here in a second," Rhonda replied. "Well, I'm here. I'm downstairs. Would you like for me to come up or would you rather come down," he asked? "I think we better come down," Rhonda said. "Ok, I'll be at the bottom of the stairs," Myles replied with a smile.

"Good morning Ami, I hope it's okay that I accompany you and your mother to your friend's funeral," Myles said as Ami approached the bottom step in front of her mother. "I know this is rather hard for you, but I want to let you know I am here for you, if and when you need me," he continued. Ami grabbing him by the waist began to hug him tightly, "Thank you so much," she said, "but I'm okay, my friend is in heaven and I don't worry about her anymore, although I miss her." Myles stood in shock and hugged Ami back, "Well, I can understand that, and you probably will for a while. But we will all meet again one day," Myles said reassuringly. "Okay ladies, let's go," as they exited the door Myles stood to the side, waiting for them to pass him, allowing the door to close behind him.

On the way to the funeral there wasn't much conversation. Rhonda was still a little nervous because this was the first time she'd been with Myles in his car. Making sure to breathe slowly, she looked around, noticing the nice leather seats, which were super soft. As she continued looking around eyeing all the bells and whistles, she thought about her clunker and how he would probably never ride in it. She started to wonder to herself if she was beneath him and if he was well out of her league.

They arrived at the church and everyone was weeping and sad. Rhonda wasn't sure if this would be harder for her than it would be for Ami. Ami noticed Kiana's mother sitting at the front, in the first pew. She turned back to Rhonda, "Mommy can we go say hi?" Rhonda assured Ami that it was fine, grabbed her by the hand and began to walk towards the front of the church. As they approached, Rhonda saw a beautiful long-haired, light-skinned woman sitting at the front with her legs crossed, looking very strong and stout. Doubt begin to creep into her mind as to how something so tragic could happen to someone so beautiful and well put together, then she began to remember her life and how something almost as tragic had happened to her. She took a deep breath. She could feel her heart melting, imagining if this was her and that she had lost Ami.

Kianna's mother noticed Ami and Rhonda approaching and stood to her feet to greet them both. Rhonda began to speak, "I'm so sorry for your loss. My name is Rhonda," she said, as she extended her hand. "Hello, I'm Stacey, and I know who you are. This must be Ami," she continued as she grabbed Rhonda's hand looking toward Ami. "Thank you so very much, I know you were my baby's dearest friend, she talked about you all the time." "Yes ma'am," Ami answered. "Would it be alright if Ami sat with me during service? I know how close they were, and I just feel like she is a part of my family," she said as tears began to fill her eyes. "Yes, that would be fine," Rhonda said, since she knew in her heart Ami needed this just as much.

"You can sit here too if you'd like," she said as she tried to make room. "No, that's alright. I'm sorry, this is my friend Myles," Rhonda said as she stepped a little to the left, allowing her to see Myles, then noticing Michelle, Raymond and the girls where standing right behind Myles. "Oh, and this is my family, my sister, Michelle, my brother, Raymond and my nieces, Stacey and Gail. Thank you all so much for coming," Stacey said as they shook hands, unable to take her eyes off Ami most of the greeting. "We're going to let you have some time with Ami, we will be in the overflow area," Myles said as they all turned and walked to the middle of the aisle.

Ami sat next to Kiana's mother, grabbed her hand, leaned over and began to talk to her. Rhonda returned with Myles and sat next to Michelle as she watched Ami talking to

Stacey the entire time. No one said a word to Rhonda as she watched, it was as if everyone knew what time it was, grief can make people do strange things, and Rhonda was not about to take her eyes off Ami and neither were they, including Myles.

Rhonda noticed the lady looking intensely at Ami, as though she was agreeing with everything Ami said, but the look on her face was as though Ami was giving her instructions. Kiana's mother nodded her head in agreement lifted her head high and pushed herself back in the seat for some reason. Rhonda now wondered to herself that Stacey looked even stronger in that moment. Myles was watching her also, in amazement. As Rhonda and Myles both looked on, they wondered what Ami could have possibly said to her to give her so much strength.

The service was now over and it went as well as to be expected. Everyone now exited to their cars. Kiana's mother was unwilling to allow anyone outside of the family to attend the actual burial of her daughter at the gravesite. Everyone was quiet the ride home. Myles and Rhonda both wondered what Ami had said to Kiana's mother. Rhonda finally broke the silence, "Ami, when you were talking to Kiana's mother, what did you say to her?" "Nothing really mommy," Ami said as she looked out the window. "You must've said something," Myles said. Rhonda looked at him quickly, realizing in that moment he was just as curious as she was. "I just told her what God told me to tell her," Ami said. "Huh, what did He tell her or tell you to tell her," Rhonda asked in disbelief. "He just told me to tell her, He had a plan for her and that nothing was lost, and Kiana was with him," Ami said in an unconcerned tone as if this was something normal.

Myles giggled a little to himself, he knew exactly what this was. Rhonda was in complete shock. She could not believe the things Ami was saying. Rhonda sat quietly the rest of the ride. She was starting to be really concerned about Ami, but she didn't want to let on. Myles tried to change the subject, asking if anyone was hungry and invited them both to have brunch with him. Ami became excited, sitting forward in the seat, "Yes, mommy please." "Okay, but you need to put that seatbelt on young lady," Rhonda said as if she was unsure. She wanted to go knowing in her heart it was all she wanted to do. "Mommy can auntie Michelle and Uncle come to eat with us," Ami questioned? "I don't know honey, Myles are you comfortable with them coming," Rhonda asked. "Yes of course, you're referring to the couple who was at the funeral," Myles inquired. "I think it would be great if you invited them, I was thinking *The Birds Café*, on 12th street id that is ok," Myles asked?. "We love that place," Rhonda said, Ami nodded her head in agreement. "Let me just call them really quickly, I'm sure they will come," Rhonda said as she dialed the number. Myles turned to head in the direction of the restaurant.

Pulling into the parking lot and exiting the car ,Rhonda saw Michelle and Raymond pulling into park, too. They stood waiting for them to catch up to them. "Hey Girl!" Michelle sang from across the parking lot. "Hey Dr. Myles!" She continued as she and Raymond approached with their twin nieces. Myles chuckled a little to himself. Rhonda could tell Myles liked Michelle already. "Hey Michelle, hey guys," Rhonda said as she grabbed the girls to hug them both and turned and kissed Raymond on the cheek. Myles thought to himself, "I hope I get a kiss on the cheek when we meet next time," letting out a giggle to himself. "What," Rhonda questioned? "Girl he was probably thinking about you kissing everybody but him," Michelle said with a laugh.

Rhonda, completely in shock, quickly caught a glimpse of Myles large smile from ear to ear. "Girl, I don't know why you making that man wait so long for some of that sugar," Michelle said as she passed Myles and tapped him on the shoulder, "Don't worry Myles, I'm here to help you out!" Raymond laughed the entire time, knowing this was going to be a fun time, if he knew his wife. "Myles this is my sister/best friend Michelle and my brother/best friend Raymond, these are their nieces Stacey and Gail," Rhonda said she tried to refrain from laughing at Michelle.

"I am very pleased to meet you all, especially you Michelle," Myles said as he held the door open for everyone. "I've been looking for someone who can give me all the secrets to winning this one's heart." "Honey from my view I think you're well on your way, if you are asking me," Michelle said under her breath as she entered the restaurant. "Oh, really," Myles said as he followed everyone into the establishment, "You must tell me more."

"Wasn't that a lovely service," Rhonda asked as she quickly tried to change the subject? Ami and the twins caught up in their own little world, followed along with the adults, chattering away among themselves.

The waitress carefully positioned everyone at two tables, the children at one and the adults at another as Ami had requested in the car. Rhonda felt it was alright but tried her best to keep an eye on her, given the events of the day. Myles assured her that Ami seemed to be handling the loss very well and even inquired with the two of them about maybe talking to a spiritual counselor if needed. Everyone seated, Michelle began to inquire, "Myles are you coming to Ami's birthday party at our house tomorrow?" Rhonda immediately realized that she had forgotten all about it and quickly looked up from the menu at Myles's face. Myles completely shocked that he was being asked by Michelle and not Rhonda, said "I'm not sure, am I invited, Rhonda?" He questioned with raised brows. "Um, yes if you can make it," Rhonda said as she looked Myles in the eyes, hoping to sense if he was really interested in coming or just being polite. "I am off until late night, I'm sure I can stop in for a few," he replied.

"Great, we will see you after service tomorrow," Michelle said, knowing Rhonda would never have asked him on her own. Rhonda smiling glancing over at Ami, who was staring at the adult table with a big Kool-Aid grin on her face. Raymond finally joined into the conversation, "Good, you can help me with the grill, you do grill don't you," he asked as if Myles's answer was a male rite of passage. "Man, I don't fool with dudes who don't, I will even bring a few steaks if you will allow me," Myles said with his strong male tone.

Rhonda and Michelle giggled to themselves. They could tell Raymond liked Myles and that was something he didn't do very often, but in truth, he was listening to see what type of man Myles was, the entire time. Michelle knew that if he didn't care for Myles, he would not speak a word until he spoke to Rhonda, whom he truly considered a sister he wanted to protect, about Myles and what he perceived of him after.

After a lovely morning Myles dropped Rhonda and Ami home and left to rest before work that evening. On the car ride home, each expressed what a wonderful time they had and how they enjoyed the laughter. Both Myles and Rhonda felt as though they had been around each other for years. By the time anyone had noticed, it was late afternoon, time had flown by and no one really wanted to leave the restaurant. "Well, I will see you both tomorrow at service," Myles questioned? "Yes," Ami answering before Rhonda had a chance, "Yes," Rhonda replied looking at Ami with a grin.

"I'm going to consider this excitement all about Jesus and not the fact it's going to be your birthday tomorrow," Rhonda said with a smile. "Or, the fact you get to see Mr. Myles again three days in a row, huh Mommy," Ami said as she snatched off laughing towards the front door of the complex. "What? I can't believe she just said that," Rhonda said with a huge guilty smile. Myles chuckled out loud looked to see Ami, then quickly turned his look in Rhonda's direction, hoping what Ami said was truth. "Alright, go on get out of here, now that you have my truth revealed by Ami," Rhonda said sarcastically, yet, still smiling. "Oh, I'm aiming for more than your truth, but I will take this as a win," Myles said with excitement as he began to put the car in gear.

Rhonda smiled all the way up the stairs and into her apartment where Ami was waiting with a grin. "Did y'all kiss," she questioned? "You are just in rare form young lady. No, we did not. We are not married," Rhonda replied. "Don't you have something to do like homework or something," Rhonda laughingly stated.

"Wait, before you go, I wanted to talk to you about your birthday," Rhonda stated now, serious in tone. I know you really wanted a bike for your birthday, yes I got all your hints, but with the hospital bills and all, I had to keep it a little more need-based," Rhonda concluded. "It's ok Mommy, I knew it would be hard and I am ok without one, maybe for Christmas or something. Besides I wanted to ride with Kianna too," Ami said with a look as though she had lost some joy in it. "Well baby, one day this won't be so painful for you, and remember we are living our best life. Now come on, let's get your breathing treatment, we are past time."

HERE WE GO

"Good Morning Rhonda," a voice said from the back of the pew. Rhonda and Ami turned to look at the same time, "Good morning Mrs. Johnson"! Rhonda, with delight, reached for her purse and made room for her to sit next to Ami as usual. "I think it's about time you called me Helen, don't you," Mrs. Johnson questioned with a smile as she stared straight ahead. Rhonda completely baffled, turned to look at Ami who had the biggest grin on her face she had ever seen. "Does that mean I can call you G-Ma," Ami asked hurriedly. "Ami!" Rhonda interrupted. "Only if your mother calls me Helen, I mean if that's ok with her, seeing as how we going to funerals and birthday parties these days."

"Oh Lord, here we go," Rhonda said under her breath. "You're coming to my party too," Ami said with excitement? "I don't know, I, wasn't invited," Mrs. Johnson said sarcastically rolling her eyes continuing to stare straight ahead. Rhonda rolled her eyes, "Of course you're invited." "Well now, that's settled. And now that I have gotten my aught right with my neighbor, I can worship the Lord!" Rhonda threw her hands up, "Oh my word," she said under her breath. Ami laughed at the two of them, glancing back and forth. She couldn't help thinking that Mrs. Johnson would be the perfect grandmother.

As service went on Rhonda, couldn't help but wonder what God was saying to her, when the pastor stood after the sermon and asked if there was anyone who needed God to heal their past and allow them to have a better future. She could think of a lot of things God could heal in her past, things she could never mention to anyone but Michelle at this point and God, Himself. She thought about the years Ami had been without a real family connection and a father. Wondering to herself if Myles was a blessing and how soon she would have before she had to share her past with him or if she even needed to at all. The main objective was to keep Ami and herself safe and it was safe for them at this point. This left her feeling as though she could move forward and she didn't feel worried like she did before, there was a peace she knew now, and she also knew it was a gift from God.

As service let out, she spotted Myles sitting in his usual spot. Making their way over to him, "Why didn't you come and sit with us," she asked. "I wasn't sure you were ready for that yet," he said. "Well she was ready for funerals and parties, why not sitting together," Mrs. Johnson interjected into the conversation, grabbing Myles to hug him. Rhonda again mumbled under her breath, "Just don't know how to let it go." "I heard that. I'm riding with you to the party son," she said as she released her hold on Myles. "Ok...,"

Myles said, looking at Rhonda confused.

"I'll meet you at my house, I hope you brought a change of clothes, you will burn up in that slick man's suit," she said as she walked away. "Your Momma is crazy, you know that don't you, and in the house of the Lord, too," Rhonda whispered as they began to laugh. "You have the address right," Rhonda said still shaking her head at Mrs. Johnson. "Yes, I'm going to stop by mom's and then be on my way. "Ok, we'll see you in a few minutes then," Rhonda said as she grabbed the back of Ami's shoulders with both hands and guided her forward.

"Hey Girl, Happy Birthday Ami!" Michelle said as everyone else chimed in with birthday greetings. "Girl, did we really invite this many people, it's over one hundred people in here and outside," Rhonda said as she made her way to the kitchen to bring in more dishes of food, gifts and bags full of prizes. "Now you know it's not that many, maybe ninety-nine though," Michelle said as she chuckled. "Yeah, and they all on my lawn too, "Raymond said as he carried the rest of the bags into the kitchen and sat them down. Rhonda and Michelle both widened their eyes at his tone and words, they knew they would be hearing about the grass for weeks to come.

"Girl, I really like this Dr. Myles character, he seems really down to earth and he is digging you!" "There ya'll go with the girl talk, I'm going to get out of here before it gets too deep cause I still can't swim in those waters no matter how old I get," Raymond said as he vacated the kitchen area headed toward the patio. "No, stay, Raymond, I need your male perspective," Rhonda yelled as he hurried away. "No, you don't, if he was a clown, I would have already told you," Raymond yelled back as he slid the patio screen closed. "Well, I guess that's that," Rhonda said as Michelle and she looked at each other with raised brows.

"What time is he getting here," Michelle asked? "He?," Rhonda said with a grin. "What you mean, he" Michelle looking at Rhonda with confusion on her face. "*He* is not coming alone, is what I mean by *he*," Rhonda said sarcastically. "Well who else is he bringing because you don't know anybody else, he knows, so…." Michelle said as she looked at Rhonda. "Mrs. Johnson," they both said at the same time in unbelief. "Girl how did you happen to invite Mrs. Johnson" Michelle questioned, in the "girlfriend" tone she used as if it was some juicy gossip? "I didn't and it's a long story. Let's just say she was not going to be left out and has insisted I call her by her first name!" "Girl that lady is a trip, from what you are telling me," Michelle said, as she giggled to herself, placing more finger foods on the tray she was preparing.

"That's not even the kicker, girl. Ami asked if she could call "Helen," G-Ma!" Rhonda said shaking her head. "What did you say," Michelle asked in shock? "I didn't have the chance to say anything the conversation was totally one sided at that point. I think I was just in shock that it was even happening and at church of all places," Rhonda continued.

As they continued to prepare for the other guests to arrive, Rhonda and Michelle continued to take the food and other items out to the backyard, where Raymond had meticulously positioned tables, chairs and other items needed for the party. Everything was so beautifully arranged that Rhonda was almost brought to tears. She could not help but thank God for placing such wonderful people in their lives. Although they were not her real family they surely came close. She began to wonder what things would be like if her mother and sister where there. She knew in her heart they missed her and wondered about them more than she cared to think about at that moment because she knew it would send her into an emotional frenzy.

The guests began to arrive, and the backyard was becoming more populated than Rhonda had ever imagined. Between all the children Ami invited and her co-workers and new church friends, Michelle knew Ami felt really loved. "Where are we putting all the gifts," Greg asked as he hugged Ami and walked over to great everyone. "Hey Greg, nice to see you out of the uniform," Michelle said as she pointed to the table beside the gazebo. "Yeah, I get the chance to hang out today. Glad we are closed on Sunday's," Greg said as she walked towards the table.

"Hey everybody," Sam said as he walked out the patio door and made his way over to Raymond at the grill. "Girl you invited Sam," Michelle asked as she turned quickly to Rhonda in unbelief? "Yeah, what was I to do? He walked up creepin' in the background when I was telling Greg and all the others to come over today, what was I going to say oh, not you Sam," Rhonda said. "Well it might have saved you from what's going to happen on Monday when he see Myles walk up in here with his tall fine chocolate, muscular, white teeth havin.....," "Ok that's enough, them teeth though... right..." Rhonda interrupted as Michelle laughed. "I'm just saying," Michelle concluded.

"Hey, where is everybody at," Rhonda recognized the voice, turned suddenly to look. "Well here we go, I'm just saying. Get ready for that mean pouty disposition on Monday because you know it's coming," Michelle concluded. "Hush," Rhonda said sharply as they both giggled to themselves. "Hey, you guys made it," Rhonda said loudly as she made her way over to grab some of the things Mrs. Johnson was holding. Rhonda could not believe her eyes, there where so many bags as if she had been planning for this day for a while. She could not have shopped and packaged all these gifts in this short of a time. "G-Ma," Rhonda heard from across the yard. "Hey, Suga'," Mrs. Johnson said as Ami ran up and hugged her, then she hugged Myles. Rhonda's mouth was wide open. "You might want to close that," Michelle whispered softly in her ear as she grabbed some of the items from them and started to walk away laughing.

"G-Ma, come and meet my sisters," Ami said as she grabbed Mrs. Johnson's hand and began to pull her away. "Hang on Ami, I have a surprise for you," Myles said as he walked back into the house, looking back to make sure Ami waited. Rhonda was in complete shock at the situation, unable to completely close her mouth at this point. Michelle made her way back over to them as they had grabbed everyone's attention and knowing that everyone wanted to know what he had gone back into the house to retrieve. Myles bent over slightly as he made his way out the door sideways, pushing a purple chromed bike through the doorway.

"Oh, my God," Rhonda yelled as Ami began screaming with excitement! "My bike, my bike!" Ami began to chant as he continued to push the bike toward her. "How did you know she wanted a bike; she didn't ask you did she," Rhonda said, mouth still wide open. "I told you to close that," Michelle said as she walked over to Mrs. Johnson and grabbed the remaining bags to place on the gift table. "No, she didn't ask me, I prayed about it and this is what I felt God said to get her, along with this color," Myles said as he let the bike go. He grabbed Rhonda, pulled her to him and hugged her. Everyone stared at the two of them, even Sam could not help but stare.

Rhonda took Myles and Mrs. Johnson around to everyone to introduce them. Everyone could tell there was something special going on between them and noticed how laid back and down to earth the two of them were, especially Sam. Before the evening was over Sam had asked so many questions of Myles, he himself couldn't help but like him. After everyone had fixed their plates Michelle,

Raymond and a few others joined Rhonda, Myles and Mrs. Johnson at a table. Everyone was eating and enjoying the conversations, laughing and having a good time.

"I had the chance to talk to the new neighbor I was telling you about a while ago," Mrs. Johnson said. "I saw him talking to Ami the other day again and I stepped out and told Ami to go on upstairs. Then I asked him what his fascination was with Ami or was he just fascinated with children, because he could be anybody, you know," Mrs. Johnson said. "What, she knows better than talking to strangers, I haven't talked to her yet, but I will later this evening, but Ami is usually a very good judge of character."

"Who are we talking about?" Myles interrupted Rhonda in mid-sentence. "Our neighbor who has been paying a little too much attention to Ami over the last few months," Mrs. Johnson said in a very frustrated tone. "Well, I think I may have a talk with him and feel him out myself, but I think you need to have a talk with Ami just to be on the safe side," Myles said in an authoritative voice. Rhonda didn't mind his intrusiveness, it felt good having people who felt like family looking out for Ami and her for a change. Besides she knew Myles and his mother only wanted to protect Ami and she was obliged for the help.

Shaking the conversation off, Rhonda turned as Michelle tapped Rhonda and asked if she was ready to have the cake brought out. Both Rhonda and Michelle stood and walked towards the house to prepare the cake with candles. "Did I just hear Myles regulate the situation," Michelle said as she opened the patio door. "Girl, I am liking this man, he doesn't hold back when he is concerned, at all," Rhonda said as she nodded her head up and down.

"Seems to me you done found you a husbandman," Michelle said. "What do you mean by that," Rhonda asked. "I mean, like a Boaz type dude, who is looking for a wife and knows his role as the man, he protects and provides, and not insecure, doesn't have to control a women, he just steps into place and controls the dome, is what I mean," Michelle concluded.

"You think he's thinking about marriage" Rhonda asked Michelle as they grabbed both ends of the large cake and lifted it from the counter? "Well he sounds like he has stepped into that role for you and Ami and from the sound of things G-Ma knows he has too," Michelle laughed as they carried the cake outside. "Girl, can you believe that," Rhonda said excitingly. "All I know is, it fits her, I mean the way she looks at Ami and you, I can tell her love is real for you guys, like a mother. And Myles, honey, that man is head over heels, that I can see a mile away," Michelle ended the conversation as they stepped out the door with the cake. "Happy Birthday to you," Rhonda and Michelle started to sing as everyone stood and started to chant the song with them.

As everyone enjoyed cake and ice cream Rhonda sat staring at all the gifts and people. Laughter filled the air as she looked around and saw everyone enjoying themselves. This was more than she had expected. Overwhelmed by the joy of the occasion Michelle walked over to the table and took a seat. "What you thinkin' about Sis," she asked? She could see the tears in Rhonda's eyes. "I'm just blown away by the love God has placed in our lives, after all these years," Rhonda said as she continued to look around.

"This is an amazing sight, and who would of thought you would begin a new chapter this full of friends and a man," Michelle said as she and Rhonda laughed. Rhonda managed to pull herself together, wiping the tears from her cheeks, "How am I going to tell Myles about James and my past? I don't even know how to bring it up or start. How will he see me if I tell him all my dirty laundry that I have held it in for so long," She said as the tears started to flow again.

"Listen Rhonda, God will show you when and how and until that time comes, enjoy your time together. This is about the now and your future, what did you say to me, live your best life," Michelle said in a demanding tone. "After all James put you through, not to mention the way you have had to live all these years through fear and running, hiding was all there was to life. You deserve to have some happiness and I'm telling you right now Myles is in your life to provide that for you and from the looks of it Ami too," Michelle said. "Now get yourself together. Here his fine tail comes now, "Michelle concluded quickly as they both laughed the conversation off, and Rhonda wiped her face and eyes again.

"Hey, you two look like y'all were having a moment. Are you ok," Myles questioned as Rhonda wiped her face with her hands and turned to look up at Myles, standing tall and handsomely over her? "Yes. Michelle was just reminding me of how blessed I am these days, just a moment of clarity for me, but I'm fine, just a little emotional is all," Rhonda responded. "Well, I think it's about time I start gathering up some of these gifts and getting them to the car, Michelle will you help me suga'," Rhonda questioned? "I'll help you too, we can place the bike in my truck, I have to take mom back to the apartment, so I will be going that way, if that's ok with you," Myles said as he pulled the chair out as Rhonda stood. Rhonda agreed with Myles quickly, "Ok, that would be great."

Gathering all the gifts Rhonda began to walk toward the car through the back yard, when suddenly she remembered Myles had never seen her car, she suddenly became overwhelmed what was he going to think when he saw her hooptie. She let the thought go as it was far too late now. Myles made his way to her, walked over while talking with Michelle. "Ok, which one is yours," he questioned. "This one right here," Rhonda replied. Myles walked over sitting some of the bags down and reached for the door.

As he tried to pull the door open, Rhonda realized it was not going to open, "Wait, there is a trick to this door, you have to pull up and then open, jiggling the door handle." "Oh, ok..," Myles said as he smiled, backing away from the door as to let Rhonda show him. "Yeah, you go ahead and take care of that and I will just watch," he said as he chuckled a bit.

Rhonda noticed he was looking at her carefully, "What? This car has gotten me through a lot," she said as she placed her bags into the back seat. "Yeah, from the looks of things it took the worst of it, but don't you worry. One day we will be laying it to rest and soon," Myles said as he placed the bags in the back seat of the car. Michelle stood by, cracking her side laughing at the two of them. She couldn't believe how freely they spoke to each other. It was as though they had been an old married couple. "Yeah, we are going to pronounce the benediction and all, and today we lay to rest," Myles continued to joke. "Oh, you got major jokes today, huh," Rhonda asked as they all continued to joke and laugh?

Continuing to gather everything and place gifts in the vehicles for transport, they found themselves laughing and enjoying the labor. "That's it, I think we have it all, Ami baby, Ami baby," Rhonda repeated. "It's time to say your goodbye's and thank everyone for coming," Rhonda spoke loudly. "Ok, Mommy," Ami said in response as she continued playing with the other children. Rhonda continued to help Michelle clean up as Myles helped Raymond and a few other men break down the tables. Mrs. Johnson had disappeared.

"Hey, where is your mom," Rhonda asked? Michelle hearing Rhonda asking Myles where his mother was blurted out, "Girl, she snuck off and is in my kitchen washing dishes!" "What?" Rhonda said laughing. "Yeah, get your mother, boy," Michelle said laughing, "She is a mess, a true mother up in here, my momma don't even wash my dishes, but she can come back anytime," Michelle said in disbelief. "My mother, on the other hand has got to step her game up," Michelle said as they all begin to laugh uncontrollably. "If you think that's something just wait till you taste that cookin', girl. You will want her to move in," Rhonda said as they all continued to laugh. Myles could not get himself together, laughing uncontrollably. He knew this was his mother's normal behavior. Somewhat embarrassed, he still found the humor in what they said, understanding they only spoke the truth.

Everything was now broken down and all the guests, now long gone, Rhonda began to say her goodbyes as Ami and Mrs. Johnson made their way to the cars, "Mommy can I ride with G-Ma and Dr. Myles," Ami asked excitedly. Rhonda still taken back by the G-Ma hesitated to try to gather herself from the shock of it, "Yes, baby, if it's ok with them, I don't see why not." "Of course, you can," Mrs. Johnson said with a smile, grabbing Ami by the hand and heading toward Myles SUV.

"We'll see you in a second. Ok, you want us to wait, make sure your car still has a heartbeat," Myles said jokingly as Raymond and Michelle both laugh out loud? "There you go with the jokes. Hush before you jinx my baby," Rhonda said as she looked at Raymond and Michelle with the evil eye. "Oh, y'all think that's so funny, don't ya," She said as she slapped Raymond on the shoulder and walked past him. "Well he does have a point, and we have been trying to make that same point for a while now," Raymond said as they all continued to laugh.

"That's ok baby, they didn't mean it. We know you're a strong willed car and you would never quit on me," she said as she rubbed the dashboard of her car and placed the key in the ignition. She said her chant in her head and started the car. "Thank you, guys, so much, I truly have no words for this. I just appreciate and love you both so much," Rhonda said as she began to close her car door, letting the window down. "Now you know it was our pleasure, we love y'all and your family, see you tomorrow sis," Michelle said as Rhonda begin to back out of the driveway, Raymond nodded his head in agreement.

DARKNESS HAS A FACE

Michelle and Rhonda only saw each other at work for quite some time except the occasional dinner invitation which most of the time included Myles. Over the next several months they would spend time at Rhonda's apartment and even received invitations to Mrs. Johnson's for dinner. Rhonda found herself feeling as though she was finally living her life and had no reservations about how God had transformed her world in such a short time. She was happy and Ami finally had people around her that she felt she could trust with Ami. Myles and she were like peas in a pod. There was nothing they didn't talk about, yet somehow with all of the conversations she never could bring herself to tell him the details of her marriage. All he knew was she had been married and it ended badly.

No matter how many times she tried to find a way to tell him, something would happen, or they would be interrupted by someone. After a while she didn't feel the need to go into the details, after all this was about her future and not her past. She finally had something real and it felt wonderful, too wonderful to include the shame and hurt of her past.

"Girl I think after all these months, Sam is finally getting over Myles and I being together. He finally spoke to me first today," Rhonda said as she walked into her office. "Girl does he have a choice? Myles only stops by here once a week and sends flowers every other week. Who could not have to come to terms," Michelle said as she walked over and sat in the chair.

"Has he kissed you yet? It's been six months or more since Ami's party. What is he waiting on?" Michelle asked in frustration as Rhonda shook her head no. "Girl, I am just happy to be with him and get to know him, we have so much fun and the conversation is so real and intimate. Neither of us even thinks about all that," Rhonda said as she closed the cabinet drawer and sat in her chair. "I don't know how you cannot think about it with all that chocolate in front of you, not to mention that darn smile, it's enough to melt the Himalayas."

"Have you told him about James yet," Michelle asked? "Every time we start talking about my past I just can't find a way to tell him. It's like something stops me or someone will interrupt us. All he knows is that I was married and at this point I don't think he thinks it is something that even matters," Rhonda said as she fixed the papers on her desk.

"Myles is more concerned with getting to know me and Ami and who we are. He asked about my family a lot. I talked to him about my mom and my sister and others in my family," she said as she began to feel the pain of being separated from them. "He asked when we would take a trip to meet them. I just kind of blew it off and said one day, but really I don't know what to say. It's just so overwhelming to even think about it and I can tell he can sense something is wrong when I talk about them the way I do," Rhonda finished. "Well I think if it is for you to tell him, God will lead you in the right time and place to do it, but until then, what about this kissing situation?" Michelle asked as she tried to change the mood.

"Girl, believe it or not Myles is not that type of man, he really loves God, and you wouldn't know it just by talking to him, but he is not trying to offend God in any way, and that includes ya' little lusty Kissin'," Rhonda said as she giggled at Michelle's shock. "Well you better watch that cause he may have one broke leg and you don't know it, till it's too late, is all I'm saying. I mean no passion at all," Michelle said as she turned her body in the chair. "Girl hush and get yo' nasty tail out my office," Rhonda said as she pointed toward the door. "I'm just telling you, the man ain't kissed you, what else is not working?" Michelle asked as she scurried toward the door. "Get out." Rhonda said as she laughed and balled a piece of paper up to throw at Michelle as she left laughing.

Rhonda finished her day at work and went home to help Ami with her homework. Then they both headed out to meet Myles for an early dinner. He made time in his schedule to meet them for dinner before he headed in to work a few nights a week. On the car ride over Rhonda noticed Ami was wearing a new necklace with a heart locket, "that's really pretty Ami, I haven't seen that necklace before, is that one of the pieces you got at your birthday party?" "No, I got it before, I just put it in my jewelry box and I forgot about it until yesterday when I was looking for something to wear with earrings to match," Ami explained. "You got it before? Who gave it to you, Mrs. Johnson or did Michelle give it to you? It's really pretty, does it open?" "Rhonda asked. "Yeah it opens, but they didn't give it to me, my friend downstairs gave it to me, Ami replied with innocence. "He said he wanted me to have something special and he got it for me,"

"What, who is this man, oh my God why didn't you tell me he gave you that. Why are you talking to him and I have never meet him," Rhonda continued angrily in scolding Ami as they pulled up to the restaurant? "We are going to finish this conversation later young lady; you don't take stuff from randoms and then don't even mention it to me for months. Who is he and how often does he talk to you Ami. I mean I don't understand why you would be talking to him and I have never seen him," Rhonda continued.

"Mommy, he's really nice and he just speaks and asks how I'm doing and that's it," Ami said as she opened the car door and stepped out. "We will talk about this later and I'm going to talk to him tomorrow and find out just who he is and what his agenda is. I had forgotten all about him and thought for sure you knew better," Rhonda said as they entered the restaurant.

Rhonda was furious when they approached the table where

Myles was seated. "What's wrong baby? Hey sweetie," Myles said as he grabbed Ami and pulled her to him leaning down to give her a hug keeping his eyes on Rhonda. "Ami has been talking to the guy Helen was telling us about, some months ago and he gave her a necklace just before her birthday that she failed to mention to me," Rhonda said as she grabbed her chair to sit.

"Oh, wow. Who is this guy? I had forgotten to speak with him, in fact I had forgotten all about him and his little side bar conversations with Ami," Myles said as he pushed both their chairs in and made his way to his seat. "Ami you do understand why she is so upset, right," Myles questioned? "It's your mothers' job to keep you safe and you talking to someone she has not spoken to is not safe, baby, in fact it's very dangerous talking to strangers. Baby I'm going to stop by and have a talk with him tomorrow, ok. Don't let this ruin your day, I will take care of it," Myles said firmly.

As they continued to talk and eat dinner, Rhonda glanced at the locket several times over the course of dinner. Myles and Ami laughed about her friend Marcus from school and his shenanigans throughout the day. Myles was convinced Marcus had a crush on Ami and was intrigued by Ami's descriptions of the events of her day. Rhonda managed to shake off the locket and joined in the conversation and found herself laughing so hard, tears began to fall.

A moment of silence fell over the table as they continued to giggle. "I want to ask you two something," Myles said nervously. "Yeah," Rhonda and Ami both responded in chime. "What's that," Rhonda said as he motions for two waiters to walk over, both holding raspberry sorbets in crystal glasses. "Was wondering if you guys would like some dessert," Myles said as he smiled watching the waiters place the dishes in front of them both. Ami, eager to have hers, picked up the spoon and began to dip out a spoon of the dessert.

"I love this stuff," Ami said as she took a bite. "Is this flavor ok with you guys?" Myles began to question. "Yes, it's fine, I love raspberry sorbet, too," Rhonda said, as she picked up the spoon and began to dip out a spoon full. "Well I know I feel like I know enough about you both now to pick things like this for you and take care of you both, looking out for the little things," Myles continued nervously.

Suddenly Myles rises from the table and walks over and positions himself between Ami and Rhonda. As they both have a spoon full of the sorbet in their mouths, they look up at him bringing himself eye level with the both. "I was just wondering if it would be ok for me to pick these types of little things out for you both, for the rest of our lives," he said as he dropped down to one knee and grabbed both of their hands. Rhonda was in shock, not understanding what he was asking for a moment. Ami, not really paying attention to Myles, dipped her spoon into the desert once more and pulled out a heaping spoon of the dessert. "Yes, you choose pretty good so I'm cool with it," she said as she placed the soon in her mouth. Ami was now biting down on something hard, her eyes began to widen. "What is this?" she asked as she placed her fingers in her mouth and pulled the hard object from between her teeth.

Rhonda, looked at Ami, then at Myles quickly. Once again she placed her eyes on Ami as she pulled the small ring from her mouth. "Oh, My God, Myles, really?" Rhonda yelled with excitement, quickly sliding her chair back with her legs, standing up with her mouth wide open. "Well you haven't gotten to yours yet, but yes, really," he said as he raised his eyebrows and winked at her, grabbing her other hand. "I want to know if you two will allow me to lead you, to cover you, pray for you and be a part of your family for the rest of my life," he said as he turned and took the ring from Ami, placing it on her right hand, then turned to Rhonda, "Will you two marry me," he asked as he watched Rhonda's face in fear. Rhonda was now full of tears, nodding her head, "Yes, Yes," she said as she looked at Ami. "Yes, we will marry you," Ami said, "Took you long enough to ask us," Ami said, as she laughed, looking at Rhonda waiting for her to find her ring.

"I think we better find your ring then," Myles said as he lifted the glass from the table. Rhonda still in tears managed to find the ring with her spoon and pull it to the surface. Myles placing his hand out, asked for the ring, took it and placed it on her left hand, as they both stood now embracing each other with a long hug. Rhonda realized the entire restaurant was watching and began to blush. Turning to Ami her eyes full of tears, she began to turn to thank the patrons, who had begun clapping. Trying to take her seat she noticed those clapping were people she knew, she could feel her heart flood with joy, as the tears began to flow even more. Myles and Ami began to cry as the moment had overtaken them as well. Now everyone was walking to them. She began to recognize them all, not having noticed any of them before, because she was having such a good time.

Tears began to pour from her eyes as she realized who was in attendance. She could not compose herself any longer, she was now in a full-blown sob, as Michelle and Raymond came over to hug and congratulate her. "Helen, when, oh my God, I can't believe it!" She managed to get out as she leaned over in a complete sob of emotions. Ami clapped her hands as she could not believe how happy her mother was. "Sam, what are you doing here," she said as she tried to compose herself once more. She realized all her friends from work and some of Myles friends were surrounding them. Rhonda felt so much love it took her quite some time to get herself together.

As they drove home, still in shock, Myles followed behind Rhonda and Ami to ensure they made it home safely. Rhonda could not believe the events, she kept looking at the ring and the smile on Ami's face as she held her hand up looking at the ring each time, they approached a lighted area as it had become dark. She could not believe it and she kept glancing at the ring the entire ride home. She was so full she could hardly contain herself, saying her soon to be name in her head over and over. "Mrs. Johnson, no that's his momma, "Mrs. Lacresha, Rhonda Johnson, Mrs. Rhonda Johnson, yeah that's it." She thought to herself. Pulling up to the apartment and gathering herself she noticed Myles was parking to walk them inside.

"How did you get everyone there for this," she asked as they exited the car. Myles stood, there waiting on the two of them. "They were there the entire time, just on the other side, but you were so upset when you came in you didn't even notice," he explained. Walking to the door Rhonda handed Ami the keys and directed her to go ahead and start preparing for bed as it had become very late in the evening. Myles and Rhonda continued to talk as they approached the apartment doors. Rhonda still in shock was thinking to herself, "I'm about to marry my best friend." Shaking her head in unbelief, they entered the hallway and make their way to the stairs. Rhonda turned to wish Myles a good night, stepping up a step, meeting him at eye view.

"Wow, what a night," she said as she turned around. Myles was now grabbing her around her waist and pulled her to him. Making eye contact he pulls her even closer and they embrace each other. Rhonda leaned in for a hug but Myles looked her in the eyes as he pulls her into himself, placing his lips against hers as they melt into each other, passionately kissing. Rhonda could feel her body come alive as Myles kissed her as though his heart was his mouth and he wanted to show her how much he loved her in that moment.

Finally, Rhonda thought in her head as her legs began to weaken, Myles made sure he held her up with all his strength. "Now, that is the last time I kiss you like that until I make you mine," Myles said as he pulled himself away from her. "I love you Rhonda Hodge and I want you more than I have ever wanted anyone before in my life. I can't wait to take you to my bed," he said seductively as she composed herself.

"You have no idea how long I have fought not to kiss you, with your beautiful lips staring at me all this time," he said as he fixed his clothes. "I love you too Dr. Myles Johnson," Rhonda said as she fixed her dress. Suddenly they heard a creak at the new neighbor's door. Feeling someone could be watching and knowing that Helen was definitely watching, they both looked around to make sure.

"Well, I guess that's my cue to get on out of here, huh," Myles said as he moves back from Rhonda still holding her hand walking backwards. "I will see you tomorrow, baby," he said as he let her hand slip from his. "Ok, good night baby, I love you," Rhonda said as she watched him walk to the door. "I love you, too," he said as he smiled and pushed the door open.

The next day Rhonda could not wait to see Myles. She had dreamed of his embrace and kiss all night. She didn't know if she could wait to be his wife but wanted to do all that was pleasing in the sight of God. After all, he had blessed her with, she was determined to keep it together and hold herself accountable. She knew it was time to call in reinforcements to keep her accountable now that her body was waking up to the desire she had for Myles. As she drove to work, she started thinking of what it would be like to be his wife. Ami would have a father she could trust with her and would keep them safe. She knew he was what God wanted for her and she was so happy about it.

As she walked into work everyone gathered around clapping and congratulating her, even Sam. She could not believe he had been a part of the event after all his moodiness and comments. She understood now that Sam was somewhat of her protector and cared very deeply for her, more than she knew. Later in the day she found out Myles had talked to Sam and Raymond about the proposal and it was Sam's idea to invite her coworkers.

Rhonda was blown away and thanked everyone for coming to support Ami and her in this life-changing event. She expressed they were her family and she could not have asked God for a better group of people to share in her life. As they all gathered around looking at the ring, the laughs and smiles continued all day. Sam even had Champagne served during the lunch rush to celebrate and toast Rhonda.

After a long day at work Rhonda finally made it home, and went in to talk to Ami, remembering her fear and disbelief Ami had accepted a gift from the neighbor. "Ami, honey I'm home sweetie," Rhonda said as she placed her keys on the table by the front door and made her way inside to the kitchen. "Hey Mommy," she heard from the kitchen as she placed the bags she carried in on the table. "How was your day," she said as she started to retrieve the items from the bag, while walking back and forth from the bag to the cabinets and refrigerator and placing the items in their proper place. "Come in here honey, I want to talk to you for a minute," she said as she continued to put the items away.

"Ok, just a second, I'm just finishing this math problem really quick," Ami yelled from her room. "Ok," Rhonda said as she decided how to address the necklace issue. A few moments passed and Ami came walking out from the hallway. "Hey Mommy," Ami said as she walked over and gave Rhonda a hug. "How was work?" She asked as she took a seat at the table. "Work was wonderful, everyone was so excited and just fun celebrating our engagement," she said as she smiled and pulled out the dinner, she would prepare for the two of them.

"So, tell me about this man downstairs and what he has been saying to you, Ami," she said continuing to prepare dinner. "Well, he's really nice and he just says hi most days," Ami said as she grabbed the necklace and began to play with the locket. "Well what do you know about him," Rhonda asked. "Nothing really, he's just nice and smiles at me a lot, when I'm coming in the building," Ami said as she smiled. "He told me I reminded him of his sister, one time," Ami said, "I don't think he meant anything by it, just was being nice, then he told me to make sure I lock up when I got in and I did," she said as she continued to play with her locket. "Why does he say that?" Rhonda asked..

While they continued to talk, Rhonda noticed that Ami was playing with the locket, "Well let me see that necklace. Did you put a picture in it yet? I'm going to go down and have a chat with this man. This is really bothering me," Rhonda said in frustration. As Ami walked over to show Rhonda the necklace her cellphone started to ring. She was hoping it was Myles. She rushed over to grab it from her purse.

"Hey baby, I'm down at Moms. Can you come down for a second," Myles asked from the other end of the line. "I'm speaking with Ami about the neighbor right now. Can you hang on a minute," she said as she looked back at Ami still playing with her necklace. "Actually, that's why I need you to come down. He is actually here, and I think you need to come down here," he said with an anxiousness in his voice. "Well ok, I'll be right down, then," she said in a concerned tone. "Ok, young lady, you are saved for the moment, I'm going to step downstairs and speak with Myles and Helen for a minute, let me turn this food off, shoot," she said as she continued to make her way out the door.

As Rhonda made her way down the stairs, she felt a nervousness come over her she had not felt in a while. She realized as she approached the last few steps, it was the feeling she had before and had prayed and asked God to reveal why she was having it. She had felt it was God warning her or some type of intuition, but she wasn't sure why she was suddenly feeling it again. She shook it off thought maybe she was just nervous about seeing Myles after last night. She was unsure of the rush for her to come down, maybe he had changed his mind or felt he spoke too soon. "Never mind that," she thought, "Just the enemy trying to make me uneasy."

Rhonda knocked on the door and waited, she heard only one lock turn and the door began to open. She stepped inside and noticed they were not alone. Helen had company sitting on the couch facing with his back to her. He sat talking to Helen as Myles opened the door. She stepped inside and smiled. Grabbing him and hugging him, she looked on at the man talking to Helen, leaning forward on the couch. She pulled back from Myles still looking at the man as he began to stand. Thinking to herself, "this must be the child stalker, wonder if he's as nice as Ami thinks." She watched as the man stood up and began to turn toward her slowly. Their eyes locked and she suddenly felt her legs grow weak beneath her. Now, losing control of her legs and her body, Rhonda begins to drop, "James." She whispered as she collapses. "Catch her, catch her!"

Join Rhonda in Book 2!

1. Does Rhonda's past catch up with her?

2. Do Rhonda and Myles get married?

3. Does Ami have more "gifts"?

4. What else is in store for Rhonda?

COMING SOON!

Will You Leave a Review?

Well dear reader, as you can tell, this is not The End! Are you enjoying Facing the Darkness (Rhonda's Story)? If so, please consider leaving your review? Some options are to leave a review on Amazon or on our website at www.EnhancedDNAPublishing.com/product-page/facing-the-darkness-rhonda-s-story. I do understand that Amazon has some restrictions regarding reviews so if they won't let you, please post on the website, Facebook or other social media. Spreading the word by telling others about this book in whatever way you want would be great – just spread the word. Your review doesn't have to be long. A simple "Loved it" can make a big impact.

Thank you for your on-going support.

Chane'

Denola M. Burton
Enhanced DNA Publishing
DenolaBurton@EnhancedDNA1.com
317-250-5611

Made in the USA
Coppell, TX
12 February 2021

50191306R00114